GORB IN THE SCHIZOCRATIC LINGUIVERSE

Text by J. Martin Strangeweather

Illustrations by Barbie Godoy

For Mary Rose, because a rose is a rose is a cosmos.

ISBN 978-1-54393-333-8

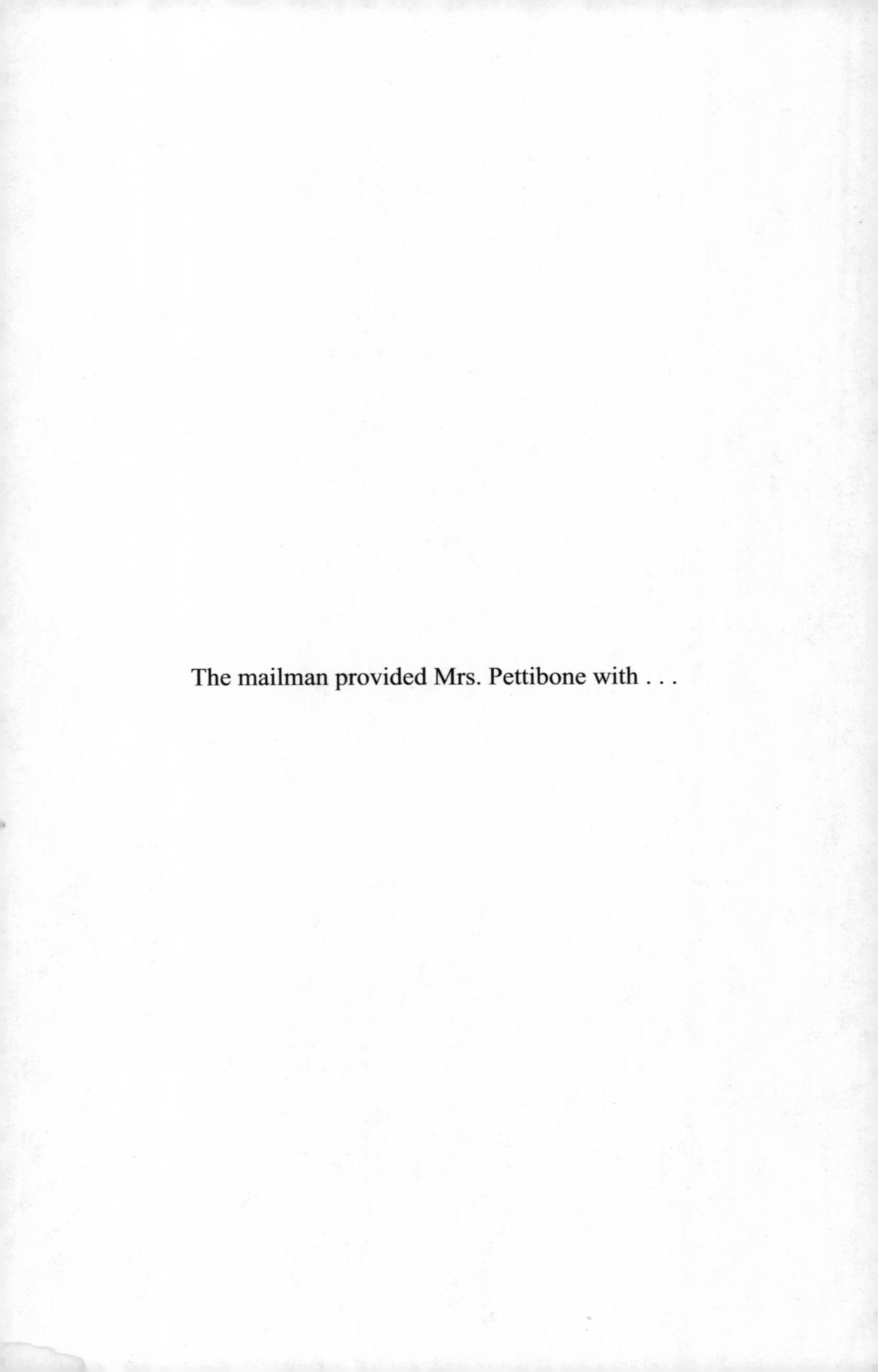

The mailman provided Mrs. Pettibone with . . .

an envelope . . .

a stamp . . .

lick here . . .

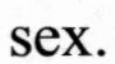

sex.

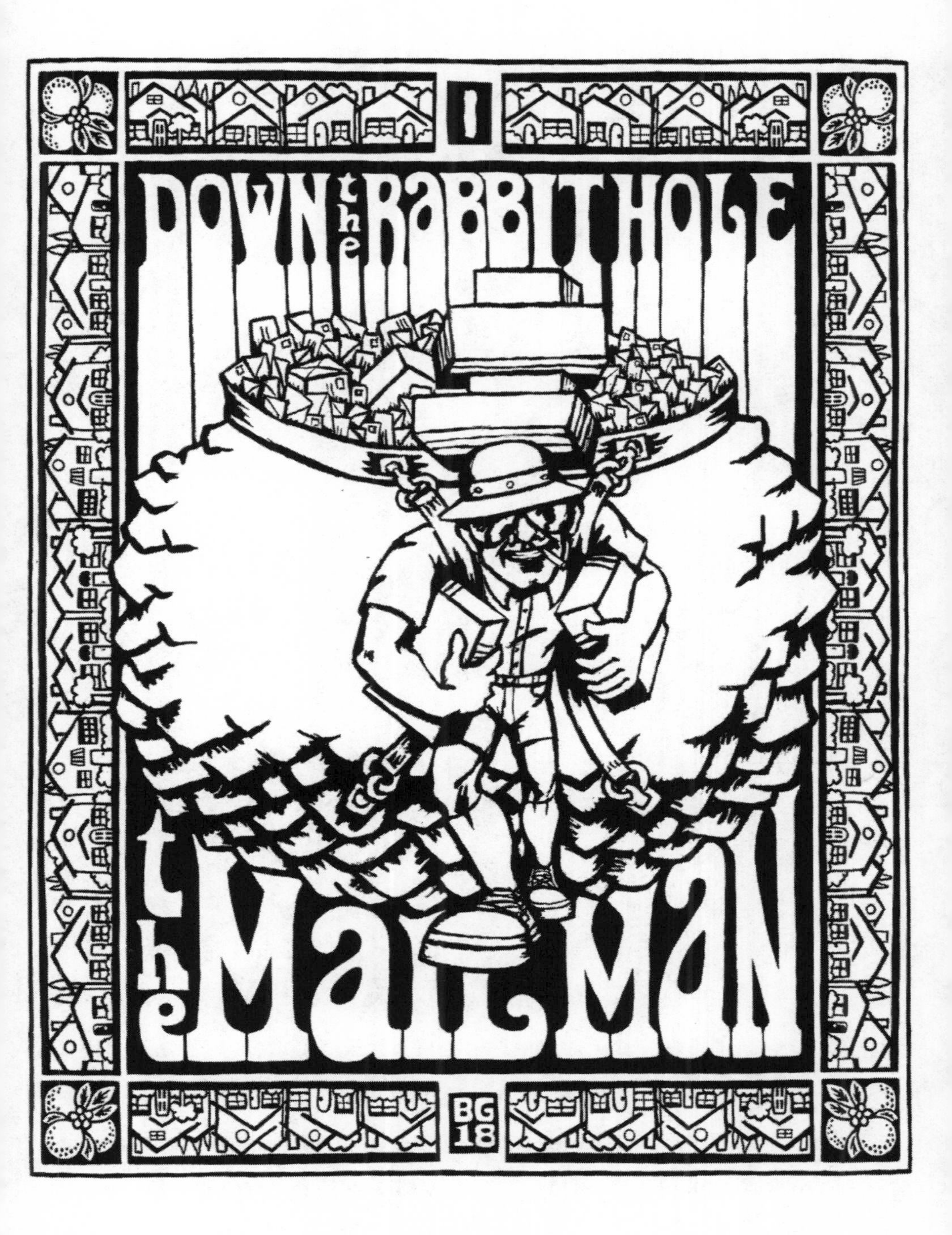
I
DOWN the RABBIT HOLE
the MAILMAN
BG 18

DOWN THE RABBIT HOLE

"You're late," said Mr. Butcherson, smoking a cigarette on the porch in his bathrobe. "Even later than usual." A butcher's son, himself a butcher.

"Is that so?" said the mailman. "I must've lost track o' time while I was busy porking your mother." He pressed his right nostril shut and blew an oystery wad out the left side of his nose, onto Mr. Butcherson's porch. "Now kindly take your package and shut that gobby cheesehole o' yours!"

"Eat me," said Mr. Butcherson, taking his package.

"That's exactly what your mother said."

The county was Orange, as was the city, and the avenue happened to be Orange, too. The mailman had packages for everyone. Deliveries that pricked up their ears and widened their eyes, made them cover their mouths while gasping and gaping and salivating for juicy morsels of daily scandal, mass-produced manifestations of desire boxed and sealed like the people to whom they were addressed. For Mr. Butterbottom, "Here you go, meathead!" For Mrs. Hiemann, "I got another package for you right here, honey pie!" grabbing his loins and thrusting his pelvis forward. For Mr. Gimpleson, who was neither the son of a gimple nor a gimple himself, "I'll bet you anything that's a big rubber kielbasa in there," shaking an unmarked brown cardboard box. "Am I right? Come on, admit it. Don't pretend. I know it. You know it. The whole town knows it. Sign here, fruitcake." For Miss Sapphos over on Walnut Street, "In case I haven't mentioned it lately," leering hungrily at her cleavage, "I'm cool with threesomes," and Mrs. Berryman on Almond, "Heard you got another bun in the oven," followed by a stealthy wink, "Maybe we should call you Mrs. Baker." For Mr. Rhoyd the grocery clerk, "Say hello to the missus for me. She's got the sweetest pair o' cantaloupes in the market. Who gives a fig if her papaya smells a bit ripe?" For Mrs. Glassman, "Sorry I'm late, cupcake. Where's that cheapskate tub o' lard hubby o' yours?"

"He's out job hunting," said Mrs. Glassman, pink curlers in her hair, avocado creamed across her face. "Probably won't be back for a couple of hours."

The mailman handed her three pieces of mail—two credit card offers and an envelope from the Department of Health and Human Services marked **URGENT**. "Tell him I haven't forgotten about the dough he still owes me from last week's poker game, and the forty bones he borrowed for that saucy little stripper from Tabasco with the fake yams, the one he told me not to spill the beans about."

Mrs. Glassman stood there silently, in the doorway, staring at the envelope marked **URGENT**. The mailman had two eggs for breakfast, and Mrs. Glassman for lunch.

Gorb looks but doesn't see. Gorb listens but doesn't hear. Gorb witnesses all of it, but only comprehends a fraction. Gorb is not he or she. Gorb is not young or old. Gorb is not rich or poor. Gorb is not ugly or attractive. Gorb is not short or tall. Gorb is not dumb or smart. Gorb is not happy or sad. Gorb merely is. No one notices Gorb walking among the hominids, observing them in their natural habitat. Gorb is too foreign for their psyches to perceive.

The local star was positioned in such a manner as to illuminate this region of the planet, unobstructed by condensed water particles hovering in the atmosphere. The dominant species had thoroughly artificialized the landscape, laying down concrete and planting steel, putting up wires everywhere. Trees could only grow where permitted. Gorb was sampling the local flora, chewing on a strip of sycamore bark. The assessment—carbonaceous and splintery. The local fauna was sampled next, first a red ant—peppery, then a cockroach—crunchy, then a bee—sting-y, after which Gorb ate a parking meter—tinny, rattly, and swarming with bacteria.

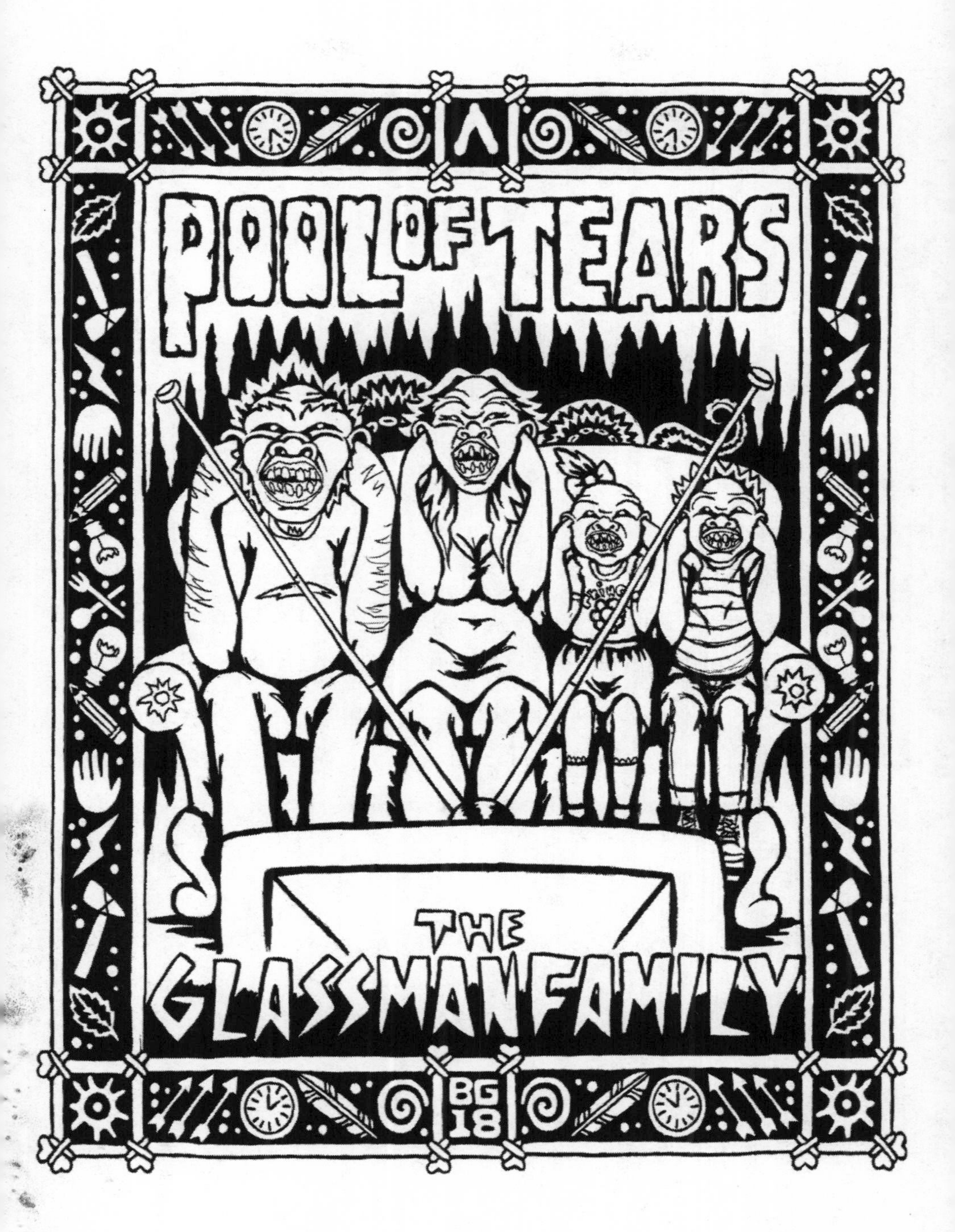
POOL OF TEARS
THE
GLASSMAN FAMILY
BG
18

THE POOL OF TEARS

Four hominids in different stages of cellular decay were sitting around a flickering picture box, staring at it in awe. Two of the hominids were heterogametic and two were homogametic. Gorb the Hyperproximal Translator studied them unseen. Gorb was attempting to translate their linguistic worlds into Floovian. Their species had advanced to the level of building artificial caves and filling them with objects that were given utilitarian names like *chair* and *clock* and *pencil* which deemphasized the astoundingly complex subatomic compositions and evolutionary histories of these objects. As the oldest hominid extracted an accumulation of coagulated mucous from his left nostril, the image on the picture box abruptly changed. A mysterious symbol flashed across the screen, accompanied by a series of apelike grunts, followed by the sound of an electronic duck.

quack... quack... quack...

The oldest hominid growled, and the four of them stuck their index fingers in their ears. This was the third electronic birdcall Gorb had witnessed come from the picture box in the span of seven hours and forty-eight minutes. The oldest hominid's reaction had been the same each time. Based on this data, Gorb calculated there was a 72.86% chance their leader was a robotic duck, and the quacking meant, "Insert your digital appendages into your audio sensors." Gorb was unfamiliar with the language of robotic ducks. Gorb was fluent in mallard and Pekin, not robotic. Floovia never mentioned anything about mechanized avians. The files were in constant need of updating.

What was the purpose of this exercise, Gorb wondered. Why would they collectively plug their audio sensors when the flickering picture box transmitted this particular signal? Was it a command? Was it a request? Would their heads explode if they refused?

Gorb filed a psionic request to the exofloovian communications division of the Floovian hive mind, asking for permission to read the minds of four related primates. The request was denied. Gorb immediately filed another psionic request to read their simian minds. Denied. Gorb filed again. Due to the high volume of requests, Gorb was put on hold.

The Glassman family was gathered in the living room watching their favorite show on television. They had no idea Gorb was studying them. An announcement from the Emergency Alert System suddenly interrupted their program. *"This is a test. For the next thirty seconds, this station will conduct a test of the Emergency Alert System. This is only a test."* The ensuing emergency alert signal sounded like a duck quacking angrily.

"Lies!" said Mr. Glassman. "There goes the government again, trying to brainwash sheeple with that godawful noise! They can't pull the wool over my eyes! It's some type of subliminal message! Plug your ears everyone! They won't tell the Glassman family what to do!"

Every episode of their favorite programming was based on the same basic formula: one un-Floovian would hide a bullet inside another un-Floovian's machinery or vent their rubbery coating with a sharp object, prompting two or more recurrent un-Floovian logicians to figure out who did it within the span of an hour, allotting for commercials.

Humans: *Homo sapiens,* descended from *Australopithecus afarensis*—each one comes equipped with a brain capable of orchestrating more than a hundred trillion synaptic firings per second, a soft-tissue nanotechnological network comprised from a hundred billion neurons, each neuron disseminating data at a rate of five to fifty transmissions per second, archaic by Floovian standards, informational surges traversing their nerves at a mere 268 miles per hour, stemming from a system of axons and dendrites amounting to over 100,000 miles of neuronal wiring. Inefficient to say the least. Creatures of wasteful design.

Schematics for Gorb's Elegantly Simple "Brain" and the Transgrammalexical Adaptor

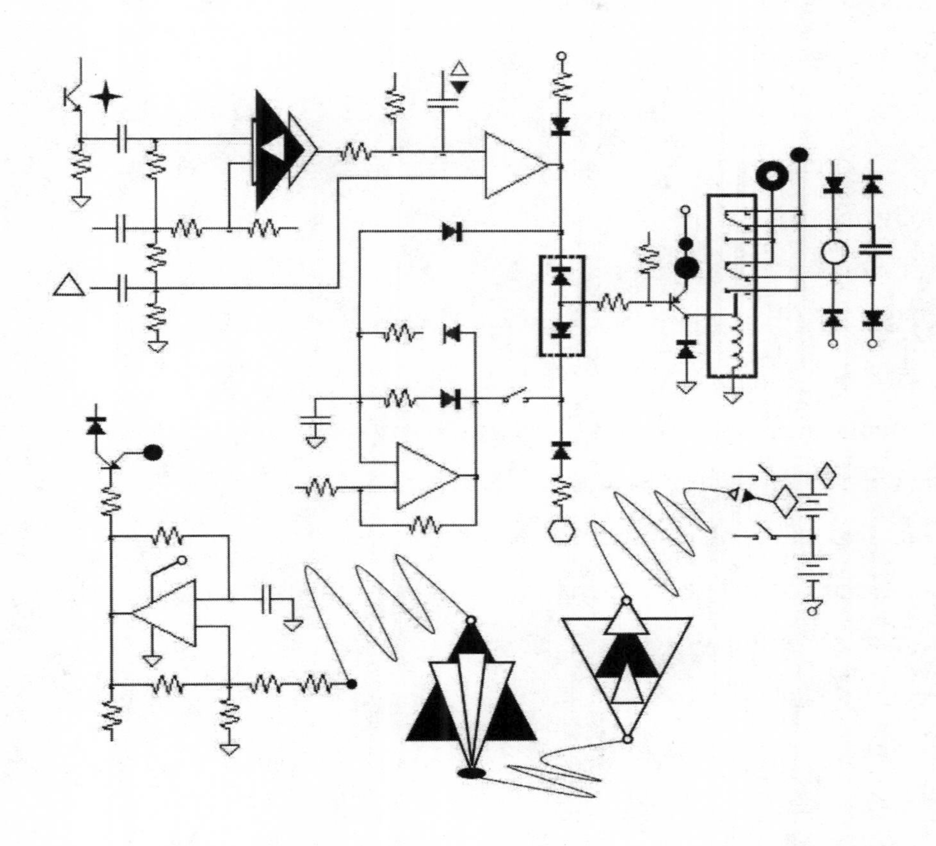

Some people see Gorb as (this). Some people see Gorb as (that). Regardless of what they see Gorb as, Gorb is what they fail to see. If nobody here can perceive Gorb, is Gorb really here? This is an un-Floovian mode of computational expenditure, tangential to Gorb's prime algorithm.

A CAUCUS RACE AND A LONG TALE
LUNCH
LUNCH
Mrs. Glassman
BG 18

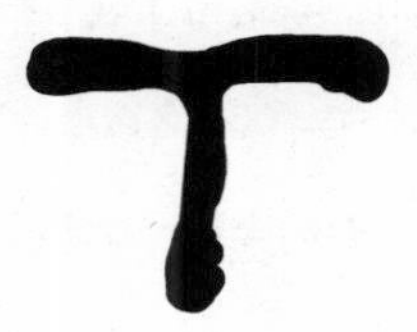

A CAUCUS RACE AND A LONG TALE

After spending a majority of the day watching television in his boxer shorts, Mr. Glassman entered the bed at 10:05 PM. He scratched his testicles for three minutes and twenty-seven seconds, during which time he considered copulating with Mrs. Glassman, and then fell asleep. He woke up for five seconds at 12:09 AM, and again at 3:37 AM due to an eighty decibel emission of his own methane and hydrogen sulfide gasses. He emitted such gasses nine times throughout the night. After putting the Glassman family children (consisting of one Charles and one Elizabeth) to bed at 10:00 PM, and collecting Mr. Glassman's six leftover beer bottles (5% ABV), and depositing Mr. Glassman's six empty beer bottles in the trashcan, and checking on the Glassman family children to make sure they were asleep, and cleaning the stovetop, clearing the dining table, and washing the dishes—one wooden mixing spoon, one mixing bowl, one measuring cup, two pots, four dinner plates, four sixteen-ounce drinking glasses, and four sets of stainless steel knives, forks, and spoons (the knives and forks hadn't been used but she washed them regardless), all of which were the "aftermath" (in her words) of a dinner she had assembled approximately four hours earlier from one box of instant mashed potatoes containing potato flakes, sodium bisulfite, BHA and citric acid (added to protect color and flavor), monoglycerides, partially hydrogenated cottonseed oil, top secret flavor, sodium acid pyrophosphate, sodium amytal, butter oil, and one box of readymade rice containing salt, hydrolyzed corn, monosodium glutamate, caramel color, corn syrup, sugar, dehydrated beef broth, mutant flavor created in a laboratory, autolyzed yeast extract, hydrolyzed gluten, disodium inosinate, disodium guanylate, phenobarbital, ferric orthophosphate, and two cans of precooked macaroni pasta containing tomato puree, beef (less than 8% crude fiber), glucose, fructose, sugar, salt, modified corn starch, corn syrup, and artificial cheese flavor—Mrs. Glassman entered the bed at 11:48 PM. The bed was a double, also called a full, consisting of one headboard assemblage (consisting of one headboard panel, one right headboard leg, and one left headboard leg), one footboard assemblage (consisting of one footboard panel, one right footboard leg, and one left footboard leg), four bed slats, four bed slat supports, four wooden plugs, two bed rails (all of the aforementioned components were made from maple, or more precisely an assortment of wood chips and sawdust mixed with glue and pressed into boards covered with paper-thin sheets of actual maple treated with a mildly toxic brominated fire retardant and phenolic resin finish [online biogeographic databases indicated the lumber had been obtained through deforestation of the Kotang region of Malaysia, forcing the relocation of a Mah Meri village consisting of three hundred and sixteen tribespeople]), twelve bolts, twelve lock washers, twelve flat washers, eight flat head screws (made from carbon steel wire plated with chromium, mined and manufactured in China [online business databases indicated the ore had been obtained from an iron mine that collapsed in 2009, crushing thirty-seven workmen {it should also be noted that ten of the bolts and five of the flat head screws contained trace amounts of blood from fifteen separate and unrelated manufacturing accidents which resulted in a total loss of three arms, eighteen fingers, and one nose, according to an online medical record database}]), fitted with a fifty-four by seventy-five inch mattress made of mildly toxic polyurethane foam and polybrominated diphenyl ether with a cotton polyester and rayon fabric ticking encasing five hundred hourglass-shaped steel coils above a box spring that was glued and stapled and stitched together by an eleven-year-old girl named Lakshmi who worked fourteen-hour shifts in Mumbai every day for three years until she collapsed from exhaustion coupled with malnutrition and expired seventy-eight hours later due to cardiac arrest (as indicated by the psychic residue contaminating her workmanship). The Glassman family housing unit had a total of fifty-eight corners positioned at 90-degree angles, six of which formed the master bedroom wherein Mrs. Glassman was resting her curlered head on a pillow made fluffy from the down and feathers of slaughtered Hungarian geese. She was remembering a time when her husband was a thoughtful lover, when he caressed her nape lightly, kissed her lips gently, touched her voluntarily, although 86.11% of the prematernal memory was contaminated with fiction. After shoving her husband over to his side of the bed, she fell asleep at 12:06 AM. Mrs. Glassman slept soundly, dreaming of sexual intercourse with five of her former boyfriends, three of her former schoolteachers, and the brother of her former best friend (none of whom with she had ever copulated, it should be noted), first one at a time, then all nine at once, an acrobatic comingling that could only be realized through the serotonin-suppressed, melatonin-saturated, oxytocin-activated, acetylcholine-motivated suspension of physics, coherency, and scruples. An alarm clock woke her up at 5:30 AM, signaling her to assemble breakfast for the Glassman family children—a heaping bowl of whole grain corn, sugar, cornmeal, corn syrup, canola and rice bran oil, cocoa processed with alkali, added color, salt, fructose, unnaturally flavorful flavor, trisodium phosphate, BHT added to preserve freshness, tricalcium phosphate, calcium carbonate, zinc, iron, sodium ascorbate, sodium pentothal, niacinamide, pyridoxine hydrochloride, riboflavin, thiamin mononitrate, palmitate, and folic acid, drenched in an opaque white fluid composed of water, recombinant growth hormones, and fatty tissues secreted by the mammary glands of a female bovine. Mrs. Glassman poured additional servings of bovine fluid into two glasses depicting the same anthropomorphized white duck half-clothed in a blue sailor outfit with a red bowtie, mixing the mammillary secretion with unsweetened cocoa powder, sugar, corn syrup, high fructose corn syrup, higher fructose corn syrup, highest fructose corn syrup in the world according to *The Guinness Book of Records*, and malt, heating the beverages to 120 degrees Fahrenheit in her microwave oven. Mrs. Glassman had been warned on several occasions by various unreliable sources but remained generally oblivious to the radiation leaking from her microwave oven, agitating the Glassman family's molecular structures at the atomic level umpteen times a day, encouraging the growth of cancerous blooms. The radiation emitted by their wireless phones was likewise harmful, as was the asbestos insulating their ceiling, and the formaldehyde outgassing from their furniture. The dirty electricity generated by their two televisions, three computers, and six fluorescent lightbulbs caused them headaches and fatigue, and the black mold in their walls gave them rashes and sore throats. The lead in their tap water was stunting the cerebral development of the Glassman family children, so was the fluoride in their toothpaste. Almost everything they ingested contained traces of the herbicide Glyphosate. Breathing their polluted air was equivalent to smoking 1.8 cigarettes a day, and the power lines above their roof facilitated the development of leukemia. Their environment was omnipresently hostile, ironic considering everything had been manufactured and purchased for the sake of contentment. While the children were making a mess of their breakfast, Mrs. Glassman prepared their lunches, each consisting of one bologna sandwich (composed of beef trimmings, water, salt, corn syrup, sodium lactate, unidentifiable artificial flavoring, dextrose, hydrolyzed beef stock, autolyzed yeast, sodium phosphates, sodium diacetate, sodium ascorbate, sodium nitrite, lithium carbonate, and paprika; the bread of which contained wheat flour, malted barley flour, niacin, reduced iron, thiamin mononitrate, dexmethylphenidate hydrochloride, riboflavin, folic acid, filtered water, salt, high fructose corn syrup, and yeast) allotted one slice of processed cheese (milk, whey, milk protein concentrate, milkfat, sodium citrate, calcium phosphate, whey protein concentrate, salt, lactic acid, sorbic acid as a preservative, cheese culture, annatto and paprika extract for color, and enzymes) flavored with mustard (distilled vinegar, water, mustard seed, salt, turmeric, dextroamphetamine sulfate, paprika, undisclosed natural flavors, and garlic powder), accompanied by four slices of green apple, one banana, and one 500-milliliter bottle of ionized mineral water. After the children had their fill of sugar, she made sure they were properly bathed and clothed with their hair properly combed and their teeth properly brushed and their shoelaces properly tied and their Ritalin properly swallowed and their backpacks properly stocked with pencils and pens and paper and erasers and pencil sharpeners and three-ring binders and schoolbooks and homework assignments before handing them their brown sack lunches and kissing their foreheads and sending them off to school by 7:30 AM. At 9:00 AM, after cleaning the bathroom and taking out the garbage and mopping the kitchen floor, Mrs. Glassman began to assemble breakfast for Mr. Glassman. At 10:00 AM, Mrs. Glassman woke up Mr. Glassman and laid out a pair of blue denim trousers along with a white long-sleeve button-down shirt in preparation for his 12:00 PM job interview. She woke him up again at 10:30 AM, and again at 10:45 AM. Mr. Glassman exited the bed at 11:28 AM. He did not shave. He did not shower. He brushed his teeth in order to mask the lingering scent of alcohol on his breath. Sans toothpaste, the tactic was only 48.52% effective. He grabbed his gray tweed flat cap and rushed out the front door of the Glassman family housing unit without consuming any of the scrambled albumen and unfertilized chicken ova paired with strips of blackened pig flesh infused with salt, sugar, corn syrup, sodium phosphate, sodium erythorbate, sodium nitrite, and hickory smoke flavor that Mrs. Glassman had assembled for him. There were dishes to wash and beds to make, and the living room had to be vacuumed before the children came home from school, and the azaleas needed watering, and she hadn't even showered yet, and the mailman would be here any minute.

Oh, the many ways to say, "I'd like to breed with you someday." Gorb's tertiary function as a hyperproximal translator is to catalogue them all. Vulbegals from the Land of Frisium in Lysanxia communicate through the loudness and odor of their flatulence, a surprisingly eloquent language. The Ronal Pronoctans who still dwell in ancient Olcadil speak a tongue so esoteric and convoluted that only rarely can they themselves understand it. The mouthless Hexalids of Elenium are fluent in the ever-shifting colors of their librium diamond eyes, graceful even when they're cursing. The hundred-armed Rohydorms of Ronlax have developed a complicated system of handshakes, pinches, pokes, and slaps to socially permissible regions of their stony anatomy. A punch in the face means the same thing to them as it does to you. Punching someone in the face has a somewhat universal meaning. The terrible Mogadons of Valaxona explode in varying degrees to express their temperaments and desires. The Shhh'ians of the twin moons Lorenin and Lorsilan have learned how to avoid communicating altogether. Some consider them the wisest beings in the omniverse.

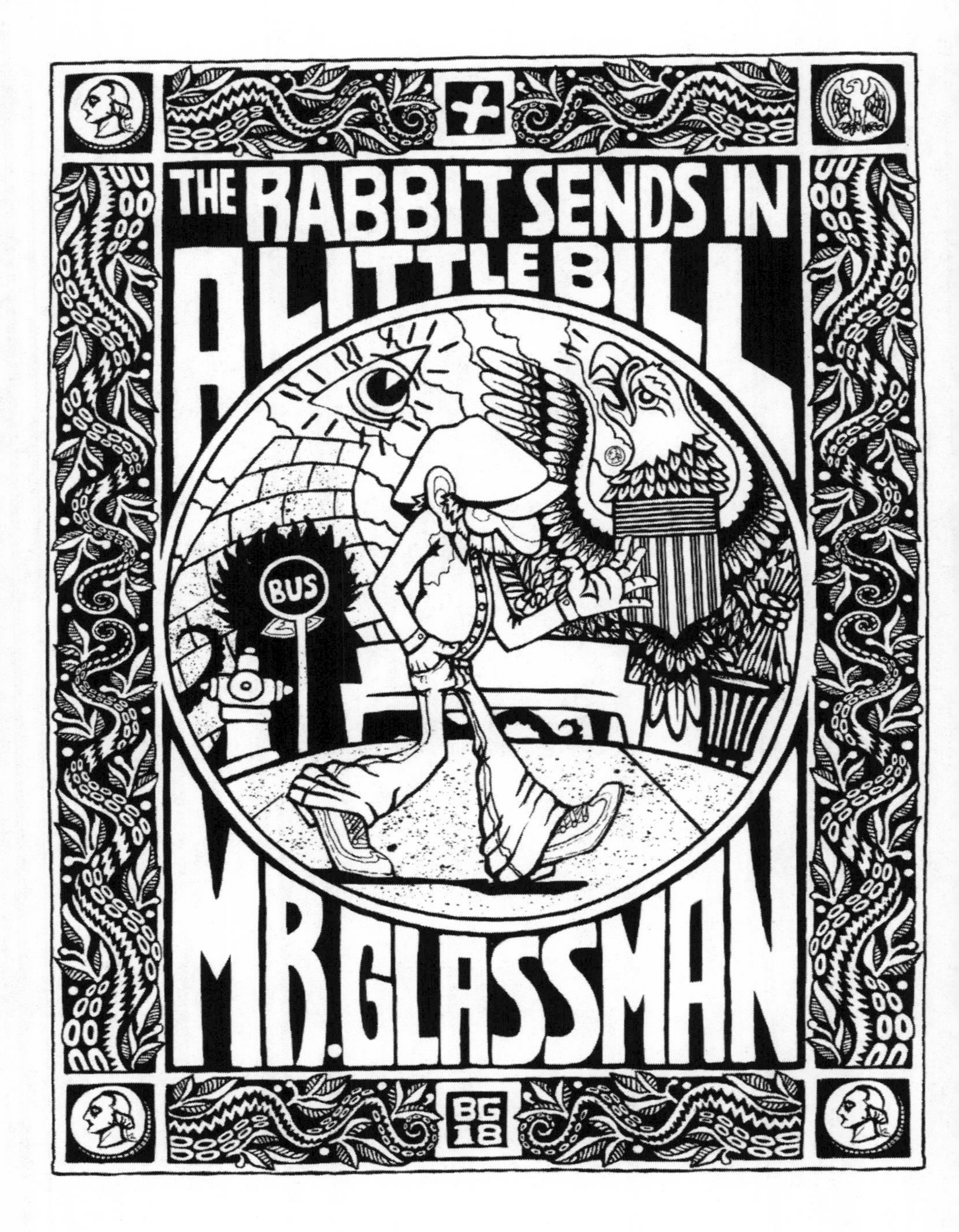
THE RABBIT SENDS IN
A LITTLE BILL
BUS
MR. GLASSMAN
BG 18

THE RABBIT SENDS IN A LITTLE BILL

Mr. William J. Glassman is under the assumption he has a special attribute called “free will”. This is based on cultural indoctrination and his ability to react to any given stimulus (for example, someone pinching him) in one of fifty-two ways (on a sober day), comparing the degree of autonomy afforded by his brain with that of a stone, or a flower, possibly a calculator—a device which can only react in one of two ways to a press of its buttons, three ways at most: it can succeed in performing the function, perform the function incorrectly, or fail to perform altogether. Gorb is programmed to react to any given stimulus in one of fifteen thousand ways, yet Gorb cannot claim to have this privileged mode of beingness called “free will”. The ability to choose from a very limited number of possible actions hardly merits the distinction of “free” anything. Mr. Glassman is not free to breathe underwater without suffering dire repercussions. Nor is he free to delete his enemies without facing severe legal consequences. He can’t in all seriousness decide to go without sleep for a month. He can't discontinue paying rent if he wants to continue living in his current home. He can't transform into a fish, or a bird, or a klugnar. He can't levitate away, or teleport to safety. He can't stop himself from staring at Mrs. Rhoyd's bosoms, or fantasizing about copulating with her. He can't stop himself from fantasizing about copulating with all sorts of women, fully aware that he's not at liberty to copulate with any of them, unless he lies to his wife, which contradicts the very notion of freedom. Owing to the shortsightedness of human subjectivity, he even believes that he's free to die. The only freedom he seems to actually possess is the freedom to believe that he's free, however erroneous.

Mr. Glassman's sole noteworthy attribute is the fact that he is the hundred billionth iteration of his species to be generated by Universal Algorithm 113BΔ of Studio Omniversal, formerly the Multiverse, a subsidiary of Studio Ultraversal, formerly Metaversal Studios. His cerebral hard drive has become infected with six hundred and fifteen malfunctioning programs, five hundred of which he intentionally downloaded.

Mr. Glassman pulled a silvery coin composed of 8.33% nickel and 91.67% copper from his pocket. "Heads to the hangman, tails to the track." He flipped the coin in the air. The coin landed face up in his palm. He reflipped the coin. "Best two out of three." Again the coin landed face up. "One more time just to be totally sure." Three heads in a row. He still debated blowing off the interview.

There was nothing random about the coin tosses. Mr. Glassman only perceived randomness due to his inability to calculate the various details involved in the process—the angle and momentum of the flip, the amount of force applied by his thumb, the velocity and rate of rotations, the weight of the coin, its size and center of mass, environmental factors such as wind speed, air temperature and level of humidity, atmospheric pressure, gravitational considerations, whether the coin was initially flipped heads up or tails up, the height of his hand upon flipping versus the height of his hand upon catching, the amount of dirt, bacteria, finger grease and any other foreign material which may have deposited on the coin's surface, and so on. Nothing was left to chance. The coin landed exactly how it should have.

There wasn't enough time to catch the bus. Mr. Glassman ran to the bus stop anyway. He cursed his legs for being too short. His pants were too long. His shoes were too small. His socks were too tight. His boxer shorts were too loose, but he said underwear was too constricting. His hat was too large. Nothing ever fit him right. Sometimes he felt too little. Other times he felt too tall. A mannequin in the storefront window reminded him that he was too unfashionable. A magazine in the newsstand reminded him that he was too unattractive. His nose was too big. His teeth were too yellow. His hair had too much gray. His penis was tiny. He always felt too fat. According to body mass index calculations he was too thin. The day was too hot. The sun too bright. His skin too pale to handle it. The bus stop bench was too hard on his ass. An advertisement for a silver Mercedes-Benz on the billboard across the street reminded him that he was too poor.

Gorb looked at Gorb's tentacles, never having had an actual reason to scrutinize them before. Were they too stripy?

Gorb was learning that the most persuasive speakers on this planet have no voice whatsoever.

ADVICE FROM A CATERPILLAR
THE APPLICANT & THE EMPLOYER
BG 18

ADVICE FROM A CATERPILLAR

Somewhere in the bureaucratic mazes of Middleville a man was puffing away on his cigar. A straight cut Claro Presidente rolled with Nicaraguan tobacco, the cigar was twenty centimeters long and fifty times the cost of a loaf of bread. (Gorb was unable to determine its exact purpose. It appeared to be an artificial proboscis capable of spewing poisonous gas, possibly to keep away dangerous animals.) A slow, relaxed draw. Ashy orange brightening with a crisp sizzle. The leathery sweetness of air-cured leaf. Watching the billow tumble dreamily to fractal wisps. The man was sitting remote as could be behind a wide mahogany desk polished twice a day to accentuate its frozen ripples of woodgrain.

Whenever the man concentrated on the woodgrain, the growth ring patterns, abstract and formless by nature, would cohere into multitudes of anguished faces wailing, gnashing their teeth, tearing out their hair, pleading for him to ease their suffering.

He took another silvery blue puff.

Gluttony enough for ten lifetimes had fattened him up, yet a routine psychic linguistic analysis revealed that his most commonly used phrase was, "I'm famished." His nose was angular, his brow was broad. His look was harsh. He had a face that was clenched as a fist. (Gorb had initially considered likening it to a puckered sphincter.) His bloodshot eyes were practically swirling as they darted around in their sockets inspecting his compact office, almost a third of which was taken up by his wide mahogany desk. He had to be sure that everything was in its place, that his microcosm of five black ink pens and two yellow no. 2 pencils and the coffee mug in which they leaned with the warning "If you can read this, you're too close", the bronze nameplate bearing his cognomen, the diamond-cut Waterford crystal ashtray, the rolodex, the *Rustic Barns of the Midwest* desktop calendar, the decorative canopic jar sculpted with the head of a jackal, the intercom phone, the round wire mesh wastebasket, all 1,008 polyester leaves of the simulated ficus, in short, every atom of his artificially lit crevice of the omniverse, was orderly. He outfitted himself in the black tailcoat and top hat of a villain from the monochromatic days of silent cinema, the kind of hyperbolic character likely to kidnap an innocent damsel and tie her up across some railroad tracks. A pointy, waxed moustache complemented the caricature. Judging his workspace to be in a maximal state of organization, the man leaned over and spoke into his intercom, “Miss Muffin, please send in the next prospective employee.”

A meek individual shuffled into his office. (Gorb recognized the meek individual. It was Mr. Glassman, except Gorb hadn’t detected meekness in Mr. Glassman until the moment he stepped into this office, whereupon his kingly title as paterfamilias had transformed to the serfdom of a minimum wage job applicant. Gorb was floating outside the window, watching, deciphering, recording. The transgrammalexical adaptor attached to Gorb’s balloonish head was set to 28% empathy, 22% symbolism, 26% subtext, 12% personification, 15% exposition, and 32% irony, with the absurdity filter working at 18% capacity. Gorb had slithered through flesh and muscle and bone and boundaries of brain to look at the scene from the employer’s perspective.) Black metal file cabinets storing the statistical histories of millions of deceased strangers were stacked from floor to ceiling, lining the office walls. Pitlike aptly described the atmosphere. (Gorb raised the empathy setting to 43%, enabling Gorb to experience Mr. Glassman’s nervousness more pronouncedly, his shame more stabbingly, his jealousy of everyone with a greater allotment of society’s goods and services than him. Gorb had to spend 14.7 seconds waiting for the nausea that accompanied these new feelings to subside. Such emotions were alien to hive-minded Floovians, who only felt functional or dysfunctional. Gorb raised the symbolism setting to 48%, with the attendant effect of Mr. Glassman’s face becoming blurry, out of focus, the color of his skin becoming less determinate. Raising the symbolism setting to 66% rendered Mr. Glassman’s individuating features indistinct, flattening him hieroglyphic. At 73% symbolism his personhood disappeared altogether. Gorb adjusted the symbolism setting to 82%, at which point:

Glassman

Glassman

Glassman

Everyman

Everyman

Everyman)

Everyman, the prospective employee, the applicant, him, he, it . . . was dressed in typical working class fashion—oxblood wingtip brogues, blue denim, and a gray tweed flat cap. Years of sacrificing now for later had wearied his face beyond its true age. His beady eyes squinted in the stark fluorescent light of the office. The employer judged his appearance to be of substandard genetic composition.

The applicant reached out to shake the employer's hand. The employer slapped his hand aside. The applicant's calloused fingers curled into knobby-knuckled bludgeons. The employer simply held out his left hand in a limp-wristed, disinterested manner, flaunting bands of diamond and gold that were cutting off circulation to his fingers. The applicant could not afford to be disrespectful. He leaned over and apprehensively kissed the signet ring shielding the employer's plump pinky, after which the employer gestured for him to take a seat on the metal folding chair facing the mahogany desk. The applicant sat down and looked the employer directly in the eyes for 2.5 seconds (to show him respect), then turned his nervous gaze to the bronze nameplate heralding the authority behind the desk as “NOT YOU!” making sure to avoid any further eye contact with him (out of respect), and removed his gray tweed flat cap (to be respectful). The applicant pulled a white mask from the concavity of his cap. Fastened with a one-size-fits-all elastic band, the mask’s vacuum-thermoformed polyvinyl chloride features were smooth and generic, anonymous. He felt less nervous after placing the mask over his face. The plastic facade smiled mirthfully, representing the comedic vein of theatre.

The employer nodded with a smirk, mashing his chewed-up cigar nubbin into a faceted crystal ashtray. He unscrewed his top hat from gelled slicks of premature gray parted down the middle. Reaching into the hat, he unearthed a black plastic mask. He had donned this mass-produced face during countless interviews. It was given to him by his former employer upon said employer’s forced retirement. The dark mask bore a scowl, portraying the tragedian. The employer knew it was just a mask. He also knew it was more than just a mask. (The employer and the applicant were unaware their masks came from the same factory in Mexico.)

The applicant took a rolled-up sheet of paper out of his cap. It was an application form. There was only one question on the application: When will you be available to start working? The applicant had sloppily penned “yesterday” in the answer box.

The employer looked inside his top hat and pulled out a pair of scissors. He grabbed the application from the prospective employee and commenced to intricately fold and cut the form. When he unfolded the application 57.3 seconds later, it resembled a chain of humanoid shapes joined hand in hand. The employer chortled as he wadded up the application and threw it into his wastebasket. Already filled to the brim with other crumpled applications, it bounced off the top and landed on the floor.

Wearing an expression of disapproval on his masked face, the employer slid a hand into his hat and pulled out another cigar. The applicant fumbled hurriedly through his shallow tweed cap until he found a lighter, then he stooped across the wide mahogany desktop separating him from gainful employment and ignited the employer's stogie. The employer approved. He took in a mouthful of smoke through the narrow breathing slot of his mask and blew it in the applicant's face. The applicant tried his best not to cough.

Leaving the cigar to smolder in his crystal ashtray, the employer shoved his hand back down into the top hat. This time he pulled out a miniature hourglass containing enough sand for a three-minute countdown (183,642 extremely fine grains, according to Gorb's calculations). He stared ominously at the applicant and placed the three-minute timer, an egg timer, on the desk. The applicant's mask kept up its jolly demeanor. Behind the mask his face was sweltering. His left eye was twitching nonstop. The keen edge of the mask's mouth hole was cutting into his lower lip. He sat motionless, watching his time run out with each tiny granule of falling sand. The hardness of the metal folding chair was irritating his prostate gland, and he suddenly became aware of an incongruent pleasantness vying with the tobacco's dominion, an aromatic undercurrent of cinnamon and cedar oil, emanating from the capacious darkness beneath the wide mahogany desk.

The employer cleared his throat, adjusting the crystal ashtray fifteen centimeters to the right, then seventeen centimeters to the left, then two centimeters to the right, restoring the ashtray to its original location. The applicant tried not to notice.

Fingers ringed golden with bonuses and commissions, tapping impatiently on the desk. The applicant didn't know how to respond. Fingers ringed golden with backroom handshakes, tapping impatiently on the desk as the timer reached its halfway point. The applicant frantically went through the contents of his gray tweed flat cap, pulling out a bottle opener and an empty box of matches, a keyring full of keys to lost locks, two stray buttons, a pen with no more ink. Fingers ringed golden with corporate downsizing, tapping impatiently on the desk as the granules ran sparse—*tap*, *tap*, *tap*, *tap*, the taps growing louder, ***tap***, ***tap***, ***tap***, ***tap***—until the applicant found the object of his meaning. He extracted from his cap a common steel nail, small and inconspicuous, but sturdy, integral to the construction of the tallest skyscrapers.

The employer pulled a hammer out of his hat (comprehending the nail's purpose in a manner consistent with the particular cogniphonic frequency he had grown accustomed to tuning into). Resigning himself to the inevitable conclusion, the applicant bowed his head. The employer set his top hat next to the miniature hourglass and took the nail away from his prospective employee. He placed the applicant's right hand on the desktop, with the palm facing upward. The applicant was breathing heavily in anticipation of the next phase of the interview. He had been interviewed many times by many different employers. Although their nameplates varied, they all wore the same demeanor.

The employer seized the opportunity to drive the nail through the applicant's palm before he could reconsider. The employer wholeheartedly enjoyed this part of the interviewing process. The prospect of inflicting pain was his only motivation for getting out of bed each morning and showing up to work. Quarterly performance evaluations, floggings for backtalk, the sharp crack of a lashing bullwhip made from hundred-dollar bills, threats of evisceration, whatever it took to build the pyramid higher. Displaying no remorse, indeed exuding just the opposite, he pounded the nail. Not just once or twice. Thrice. Three hard whacks cracking the capitate carpal, three yelps at ninety-seven decibels which betrayed the applicant's carefree mask, nailing his right hand to the mahogany desktop. (Gorb's right prolateral tentacle flinched, an empathetic reflex. Gorb was fully submerged in both of their psyches.)

The applicant tried earnestly to believe that he needed this job. His wife needed him to get this job, she told him so. His children needed him to get this job. He suffered the pain of his crucifixion with stoic dignity. The file cabinets, the wastebasket, the synthetic ficus, the intercom, the desk, the man sitting behind the desk, the tailcoat of the man sitting behind the desk, the cufflinks on the tailcoat of the man sitting behind the desk, and everything else in the office, including the office itself, the walls, the carpet, even the lights—it was all just an advertisement. Everything was advertising itself as an object of utility, of luxury, something manufactured, something bought and sold. Desired and whored, he thought to himself, the whole environment unabashedly whoring itself out, smothering him in commerce. How could he resist doing likewise? The employer allowed him a minute to compose himself. The applicant's mask maintained a cheerful facade as he tore his impaled hand away from its mooring. Blood spilled across the employer's mahogany desk. The applicant was quick to pull a rag out of his cap and wipe up the mess. He then tied the rag around his hand to stanch the bleeding.

(Gorb took the momentary lag in their communicative exchanges as an opportunity to conduct a field experiment. Turning the hexagonal dial of the symbolism setting up to 95%, the already sparse coloring of the office went totally mute. The scene became hard-edged and pixelated, dissolving into a grid of black and white squares that made characters and objects impossible to recognize or even distinguish from one another. Turning the knob slightly further to 98% had the effect of melding the black and white pixels into a smooth gradation of gray that faded to black in the very leftmost corner of Gorb's monocular field of vision and white in the very rightmost corner. At 100% everything went solid lead gray. The same thing happened when the setting was at 1%. Conclusion: inconclusive. Gorb returned the setting to 82%.)

The employer was still wearing a look of dissatisfaction. In a desperate attempt to gain favor, the applicant searched for the best representation of himself, an offering unlike any other to dazzle the jaded employer. The sky went dark. Rays of light sprang from the applicant's floppy gray cap, and he pulled out the very sun itself! Blinding radiance flooded the office, considerably raising the temperature. The plastic ficus melted almost immediately. He cupped the sun in his calloused hands and held it out for the taking, blindly stumbling forward and knocking over the canopic jar, burning down the *Rustic Barns of the Midwest* desktop calendar, scorching the rolodex unreadable. Drifting embers quickly translated all the hopeful names in the wastepaper basket to ash.

If the melted features of the employer's mask were any indication, he wasn't impressed. He reached deep into his black top hat, sticking the entire length of his arm inside and groping through its darkest recesses. The employer snickered sinisterly, pulling out a weather-beaten silver coin stamped with the image of Julius Caesar. Holding the silver coin at just the right angle, he managed to eclipse the sunlight, turning its brightness to shadow. (Gorb detected critical levels of satire while noting how a miniscule coin was enough to blot out the entire sun when positioned strategically in front of a hominid's eyes. Floovia had no use for monetary systems. It would be like paying your toe to do the work of a toe.) After that, it was a simple matter of scooping the celestial orb into his top hat, effectively smothering its brilliance. (Gorb noted that the sun was back in its place among the heavens.)

The applicant gave up (in so many ways, on so many things [the employer sensed it, and Gorb sensed it through the employer, and Floovia sensed it through Gorb]). He had nothing useful left to proffer the employer. Frustrated beyond reason, he put the only good hand he had left in his cap and pulled out a pistol. The employer's sardonic mask of tragedy came undone and fell away, exposing a visage of sniveling fear underneath. Symbolism became trivial with a hostile gun staring him between the eyes. The employer didn't remember his bank account number, or the extravagance of his savings. He didn't remember the comfort of his Corinthian leather car seats (produced in Newark, New

Jersey), or the two-hundred-dollar bottle of Dom Pérignon he'd had with dinner last night. He didn't remember the hundred-dollar plate of foie gras he'd had for lunch an hour ago (some of which was still stuck between his teeth), or the smoky taste of his fine cigar. He didn't remember being Pharaoh. He overturned his top hat, dumping out a pile of flimsy paper rectangles embellished with cryptic symbols and presidential portraits. Money no longer motivated the applicant. He fired two bullets into the employer's heart. The bullets were not a metaphor, and the employer was not a symbol. He was all too tangible. The employer remembered the single word that killed him. It was whispered by his wife six years ago as she walked out the door carrying a bundle of her clothes—

Goodbye.

The former employer slumped over on his desk, lifeless. The applicant shoved the former employer to the floor and stuffed him into the hollow under his wide mahogany desk (next to the mummified remains of two other former employers), but not before scalping his fallen nemesis of top hat and tailcoat (he tried to get the rings as well, but they were stuck on the former employer's pudgy fingers and would not budge). Handling the top hat with great reverence, he carefully placed the headgear on top of his own head, and slid the tailcoat on. The new outfit draped ill-fitting as a boy playing dress-up in dad's clothes, but the tailor would handle it soon enough. Only one thing was missing. The applicant reached under the desk and peeled off the former employer's pointy, waxed moustache. Using some glue he found in the top hat, the new employer affixed the moustache to himself and curled the hairs in a stereotypical villainous manner. He accustomed himself to the comfortable hypocrisy, letting the costume clothe his psyche. His ethics were an illusion, conveniently employed during one moment, conveniently discarded during the next. (Something didn't feel right. The symbolism setting was too high. Gorb turned it down before Gorb's translation was corrupted any further.)

It was a very fine day for Mr. Glassman. He reclined in his imperious leather chair and picked up the cigar smoldering in what was now his diamond-cut Waterford crystal ashtray. The new employer contentedly puffed away. After relaxing for a third of the el Presidente's length, he leaned over and spoke into the office intercom. "Miss Muffin, please send in the next prospective employee."

Gorb only refers to Gorb as Gorb. Only Gorb refers to Gorb as Gorb. Gorb has a sibling named Brog. Gorb and Brog are nothing alike. Their names sound completely different.

Pig and Pepper
Hard Luck Annie
BG
18

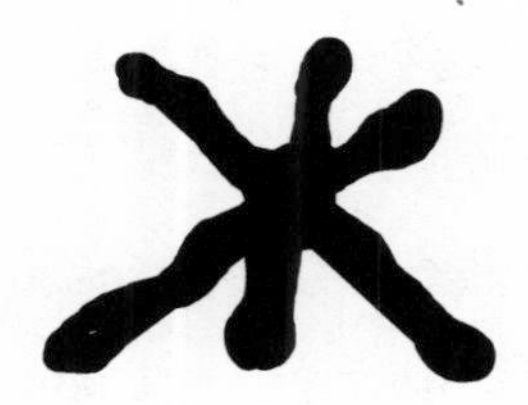

PIG AND PEPPER

Mr. Glassman left work early. “God spits out the lukewarm,” he muttered to himself, ambling along the sidewalk looking for cracks in the pavement to avoid stepping upon, forcing other pedestrians to walk around him. “Who’d want to be in His Holy Gobbler anyway? Where’s that going to get you? Chewed up and transubstantiated into a big pile of righteous Crapola, that’s where.” He pictured a great and terrible White-Skinned Hominid God gorging on pious throngs, the blood of martyrs dripping from His long Beard, not giving it a second thought as he stumbled into every beggar clotting his path, even kicking a few aside.

“Please, kind sir,” spoke a beggarly lout, “all strangers and beggars are from God, and a gift, though small, is precious.”

“For we are all beggars, each in his own way,” added his gap-toothed mate.

“Ay,” said the drunkard down the lane. “Wooly bully wishy wellers! Whiles I am a beggar I will rail and say, there is no sin but to be rich; and being rich, my virtue then shall be to say, there is no vice but beggary!

That's a dose of the old Bard. Spare a clankety and help a soul get to the other side."

"And let us not forget the words of the good book," preached another of the road's brethren, "Give strong drink to the one who is perishing, and wine to those in bitter distress; let them drink and forget their poverty and remember their misery no more."

Hwark and spittle in their outstretched palms, a polished brogue planted in their groins. With one exception. A single beggar he dare not offend, sidestepping the endomorphic female hominid and her sickly ward, doffing his cap respectfully, then flipping her a coin and saying, "God bless you, ma'am."

Something about this particular homeless hominid fascinated Gorb. Gorb filed a psionic request to study her mind at the increased capacity of Immersion Level Floop. Immersion Level Floob wasn't immersive enough, and Immersion Level Floog would prove too dangerous with a psyche this alien. The request was approved. Hers was indeed an odd pocket of the linguiverse, chock full of outdated argot and needless neologisms half-baked into otherworldly idioms and jury-rigged portmanteaus. She had developed a post-apocalyptic linguistic experience of this region of the planet—so salty, so raw, so Gorb let Mr. Glassman navigate the rest of his way home alone. This particular homeless hominid was more primal than the others. She was old and lumpy, resembling a camel leather sack overstuffed with copper cookware. Her legs were elephantine stumps barely useful for short-range shuffles. Creases of sorrow adorned her shriveled face like tribal tattoos. The locals had christened her Hard Luck Annie, but Annie wasn't her real name. She had forgotten that guise long ago. She was the saint of skid row, a beggar's beggar with a reputation for nursing broken souls, easing more than a few through their last breath. With residues of dumpster-rummaging smeared across her face, Annie proclaimed to passersby, "Rampant addiction to sugar is the demise o' this culture!" scratching at the colonies of lice taking residence in her wiry gray hair. "Free yerselves from comfort!"

In addition to studying the collectivist behavior of bees and termites and eight species of ants and orally testing various soil samples throughout the downtown area for radiation and bacteriological content and becoming familiarized with the conventions of a bewildering heterogeneity of printed and electronic modes of expression hominids rely upon to disseminate information among themselves, Gorb trailed Hard Luck Annie to the same busy street corner six days in a row and observed her begging earnestly for the bedeviled bloke (in her diction) that she had taken under her wing. Brittle bones and ebbing strength only permitted the care of one patient at a time. "I ain't a glutton fer praise," she said regarding the matter. "One act o' mercy at a time does the Lord's work just fine." Reaching astrally into her head and gliding a black-and-white-striped tentacle over the contours of her cerebral cortex, reading dendritic formations like braille, Gorb was able to assess her general lifestyle patterns. She ate what others no longer wanted, and drank what others no longer would. She was more likely to talk at you than to you. She struggled with want every other second, blinked fourteen to sixteen times a minute, took approximately eleven hundred breaths per hour, worked every day of the year including holidays and hangovers, averaged two bowel movements per week, and each month would see her with a new patient. There was never a shortage of sufferers in this "godfersunken" city. Everyone loved and admired dear old Annie, but Gorb saw more to her picture than an image projected on a chemically-treated photosensitive surface could ever display. This saint was multifaceted, not unlike the rest of the saints during their real lives. *Only in eulogies do sinners become saints.* Gorb had read this on the cover of a trifold brochure listing the weekly schedule of services offered at Mother Mary's Sacred Heart Holy Family Cathedral.

The promise of a Goodyear was lumbering through the clouds, fat as the nation. Hard Luck Annie was cruddled up against a brick wall on her favorite street corner, nestling a cripple in her arms. Cursed he seemed. His incoherent moans and gallowgurgles testifying to the nearness of a total system shutdown. He bore the look of many ethnicities congealed to tan. Blind he was, with extremities curled like wilted leaves. The poor sot was undoubtedly braindead. A mélange of snot and saliva dripped from his barnacled puss.

Annie clutched the fragile patient to her sagging bosom and raised an outstretched palm for charity, evoking a beggarly vision of the Pieta. Her facade of humility was so humble that everyone who gazed upon her felt wretched about themselves for hours afterward. The dumpy caregiver implored passersby to give whatever they could possibly spare to help her hapless friend. Locals were aware of her reputation for helping the plagued. They trusted their donations would go to her patient, and not up her nose or into her veins.

An elderly lubber wearing an Armani chainmail business suit strolled past Annie. He was taking his prize poodle for a walk. The poodle sniffed at her ragamuffin garb and proceeded to rid its bowels on the sidewalk in front of her. Annie grabbed the lubber's chainmail sleeve and barked, "Hey moneybags, quit skunkin' up my corner with yer overpriced butt sniffer!"

The lubber yanked his dog's leash, "Bad doggy!"

Annie rebuked him, "It ain't the mutt's fault! From my angle o' perspectivin' it looks like yer the bad doggy, ya buzzardy ol' fancy pants! Lettin' yerself be led 'round by the noose! Shame on ya! Flauntin' yer riches while the rest o' us flump here on the curb eatin' yer garbage! Yer glitzy duds alone could buy knickers and kickers fer half this neighborhood, and there's enough vitamineralsy poundage on yer highfalutin pooch to feed five starvin' families!"

The lubber's face turned ruddy with embarrassment. "Please madam, don't make a scene. I'm just out walking my dog. I'm not looking for any trouble."

"Yeah, I'm sure yer not lookin' fer trouble right this second, but I bet an ol' screw like yerself has caused yer fair share o' it! When I look at ya and yer pooch I see two mutts, 'cept the pooch don't know how to lie. Yer livin' proof that people ain't evolved very far from our mongrel ancestors. We still gots the beasties in our blood."

People were staring. The lubber was starting to feel uncomfortable. "Please madam," he said, brushing the literalness of Annie's grubby mittens off him, "find some other taxpayer to pick on. I'm not your enemy."

Annie snapped back, "Oh yes ya are! Yer the enemy o' anyone who wants somethin' fer nothin', ya skizzled ol' trickler! Yer never gonna escape yer enemy 'cause yer true enemy is yerself! It's the selfish beasty inside o' ya!"

The lubber threw a few coppery clanketies on the pavement to placate his verbal assailant and retreated into the thicket of sweaty bodies overcrowding these streets. "Beggar that I am," muttered Annie, "I am even poor in thanks."

This was a good day for Annie. Even her secret pockets were crammed with beggared booty. She lifted her weighty baggage of a companion and hailed a cab. Taxis clogged every street in this bustling sector of commerce, forming rivers of honking red lights and yellow painted steel. In an effort to conserve gas, Annie's driver took a shortcut, dodging oncoming traffic for ten minutes driving the wrong direction down a one-way street. The cabbie would gladly risk both of their lives to save a few bucks, and Annie respected him for it.

Annie resided in the heart of the shantytown district. She had assembled her residence from four cardboard refrigerator boxes cut open and rejoined as a single quadrangular structure with duct tape, reinforcing the corners with straightened wire hangers—five unbent wire hangers taped in a columnar bundle made a sturdy enough brace for cardboard. Three layers of trash bags stapled to the roof helped keep the rain out. Her door was a moth-eaten blanket held up by two clothespins. Upon entering, she stopped to perform the sign of the crucifixion, crossing over head and heart with two fingers crossed, then dragged in her friend and shoved him roughly to the back of the box. She spit-washed herself, concerned more with ritual than cleanliness. Minutes later she was dining on a stale donut scavenged from the dumpster outside her door, ignoring the moans and gallowgurgles of her patient. The scent of urine dominated her improvised little sanctuary. It was coming from her patient. It was also coming from the yellow plastic pee bucket in the corner, and from the dumpster next door, where she would regularly dump out the yellow plastic pee bucket. The general vicinity reeked of urine.

After dinner the old spinster hobbled to the corner liquor store and traded her coins for paper currency—two pristine hundred-dollar bills. A fifth of vodka she also bought, cheapest of the cheap rot, telling the clerk it'd ease the pain of her current ailing project. Back at her musty cardboard box, Hard Luck Annie unscrewed the liquor bottle's cap and dabbed just enough vodka around the dying man's lips to give him the stink of imbibing. She estimated by his festering whiff and labored wheezing that he only had another three days left in him.

Hard Luck Annie caressed the hundred-dollar bills as if there were something inherently precious about them, hobbling wobbly-bobbly to her toilet. Squatting over the yellow bucket, she extracted a Ziploc bag from her rectum and added the loot to an already sizable roll. After a quick slickening with lard, the bank of Hard Luck Annie was carefully reinserted. Annie commenced to pickle herself, the saint of the sewers, draining the entire bottle "lickety-splickety" in her parlance, the way water takes to sponges or problems take to paupers, dribble glistening down her double chin and apron.

Annie drank herself into a remorseless sleep like that of a babe before the emergence of conscience and its psychological checks and balances. Her partner was twitching in the corner. Used him as a pillow, she did. Whimpers, moans, gallowgurgles, guinea gasps, and his billorious gusts of flatulence soothed her almost as much as the constant hum of traffic. Gorb didn't need sleep, just like screws and screwdrivers don't need sleep. Gorb hunched over Annie's partner taking mental notes regarding the hominid process of dying, counting his breaths and heartbeats per minute until the countdown reached zero. A gurgling gasp, a sputtering outgas, and he went silent. Annie was jolted from her restfulness upon hearing a lack of any sounds associated with the struggle to survive.

Apparently she had miscalculated. Her partner died sooner than expected. "Inconvenient," she muttered. With a swift kick to the corpse's ribcage, she carkled, "Ya sorry quitter!" and spat in his face. She put on her galoshes and paced back and forth, hunching her crookedness even crookeder to avoid collision with the low cardboard ceiling, slurring curses with every step closer to the witching hour. At the stroke of midnight, heard chiming from Mother Mary's down the street, she laid out his body on butcher paper and chopped him into ten pieces using a meat cleaver and a wooden cutting board. She kept the cleaver and board in a shopping cart parked behind her cardboard shack. Wobble-wheeled and tarped in trash bags, the cart also stored one pot, one pan, one can opener, one stainless steel dog bowl, one one-gallon plastic jug for water or whatever, one Tupperware container filled with lard, one pair of tongs, one pair of scissors for cutting cardboard, hair, and throats, one flathead screwdriver that doubled as a shank, one roll of butcher paper that sometimes filled in for toilet paper, one roll of duct tape for home repairs and bandaging blistered feet, one battery-powered hot plate, one brass candlestick, one toothbrush with brownish bristles that alternated as a dish scrubber, assorted bags and blankets and strings and strips of rag, and one

Woody Woodpecker talking plush toy with stuffing coming out of the seams, its speaking mechanism inoperative. During the disassembling of her patient, she "uncorked a ditty" of her own devising: "*Chop off the mop top, chop off the arms, choppin' off the legs won't do ya no harms, chop off the hands and chop off the feet, meat is meat when yer starvin' in the street!*" She was careful not to get blood on her cardboard refuge. Refrigerator boxes were hard to come by. The dismembered contents were stuffed into a trash bag, further concealed inside a laundry sack.

Annie slung the sack over her shoulder and hailed a taxicab. Armadas of taxis bombarded the streets night and day. No one was ever safe from the homicidal driving habits of their unlicensed pilots. She ordered an unsuspecting chauffeur to haul her carcass to the local black market meat sellers. Shantytown's populace couldn't afford the luxury of factory-produced canned meat, so they sought out the shady meat hawkers—distributors of bad beef, tainted fleshes, and questionable sources of protein. As the custom went, no questions asked.

Annie slunk up to one of the burly butchers, more commonly called bone grinders, and related a mournful tale of valiance overpowered by sickness. "I did everthin' I could fer the soggy bastard, but it weren't no use. We're all meant to meet the rotter sooner or later. Gots no sympathy fer deadsies. It's the livin' I feel sorry fer." She patted the bulging laundry sack as if the chopped-up corpse inside was still her bestest matey. "It's a shame to let anythin' go to waste in these malignorant times, the Age o' Gray. Sick or whatnot, this son-of-a-gutterblood still has some decent meat on his bones. Sausages aplenty waitin' there boy, ye'll see. Damn better than a bilge rat! Fer a small price I could be persuaded to charitably donate his fleshy wares fer the good o' the poor."

"Didn't I see you sneakin' around here a few months back?" said the bone grinder.

"Shut yer gabber! No questions asked, remember?"

"Yeah, I'm sure of it. You're that one broad, ain't you?"

"What part o' *no questions asked* ain't ya gettin'?"

The bone grinder looked around to make sure nobody was watching as he discreetly handed her a twenty-dollar bill. The treasure was soon nestled snugly in her fecal coffer along with all her other capitalistic gains.

Hard Luck Annie woke up grog-blossomed in the lateness of the afternoon. She spit on the edge of her tattered apron and used it to wash her face, armpits, and crotch. Her garb consisted of an apron worn over a bathrobe worn over a muumuu, patched up with rags fastened by safety pins. She hadn't taken a bath for years, unless you counted that time she slipped from a levee and fell into the Santa Ana River.

Annie had a doozy of a hangover. Her mind was bleary, out of order, unkeen of her surroundings. Trying to hail a cab, she tripped on the curb and stumbled into the street just as a one-eyed cabdriver was screeching around the corner. The impact wasn't severe. She rolled onto his hood and rolled back off, a minor incident which left her right knee somewhat banged up and blued. Unfortunately that was her bad knee to begin with. The cyclopean cabbie apologized diplomatically, "Watch out, fat ass!" and offered Annie a free ride to wherever she wanted, after a bit of coaxing on her part. Since his cab was already full, he strapped her on top of the luggage rack, free of charge. Annie chalked it up to her epithet.

The one-eyed cabbie (technically he wasn't cycloptic; he had two eyes, but one of them was covered with an eyepatch) was such a skillful driver that he only crashed twice while rocketing Annie to her destination. The collisions were mild, owing to his skill. Annie thanked the cyclopean cabbie for his charity, "It's a miracle we're still tickin'! Learn how to drive inside the lines 'fore ya kill someone, ya roadlickin' tire biter!" And he thanked her back, "If I ever see you again lady, I'm gonna run over your fat ass twice to make sure the job is done right!" They were typical examples of the civility of civilization. After thanking the cabbie again by waving her middle finger at him, Annie thanked the Lord for safely delivering her to the supermarket.

The customers eyed her like she didn't belong. The security guard tried not to look like he was following her. The manager didn't want any problems. He'd dealt with her before. She drifted back and forth through the aisles for thirty-two minutes, eventually lugging a one-gallon bottle of lemon-scented disinfectant up to the checkout counter. She had four more items secretly tucked underneath her ragamuffin garb: a six-ounce bottle of nail polish remover, a two-ounce jar of nutmeg, a can of Chef Boyardee Beefaroni, and a nail clipper. The cashier was a tattooed baldy in her late teens with a sterling silver doorknocker hanging from the septum of her nose and a cold sore crusting chartreuse in the corner of her matte black lips. "That's poisonous, you know," she said with a smirk, scanning the barcode on the bottle of disinfectant. "You can't get drunk on it."

Annie wanted to smack the cashier in the kisser but her pudgy arms weren't long enough to reach across the checkout counter. "I know it ain't fer drinkin'! Uppity li'l vaginereal laplicker! It's fer sterilizin' my hovel, ya savvy? Gots to minimize the spread o' contagious viruses and whatnot. Flu season's a real getter this year! Gots 'em droppin' off like flies."

On her way home, Annie ducked into Mother Mary's to express her faith. Plundering coins from the collection boxes was a favorite pastime of hers. Her actions didn't go unnoticed. The priests were aware of her thefts, although they didn't seem to give a fig. Their wallets were, in her phraseology, "overfloodin' with ill-begotten greenery" anyway.

Hobbling to the exit on a swollen knee blooming purple, Annie paused at a white marble basin filled with holy water. She dipped her fingers into the aqueous sacrament and made the sign of the cross over her heart. Then she stuck her head in the basin and took a sip that turned into a slurp, figuring the Lord wouldn't want her to leave thirsty. Annie was gargling holy water as a clergyman passed by. "Doing the Lord's work as usual, eh Annie?"

She spit the blessed liquid onto the sidewalk in front of the cathedral doors. "Slag off, bungwinker!" The cathedral's 3.65-meter-tall wooden doors (3.65 meters = 12 feet, Gorb sensed meaningful correlations at work here) depicted intricately carved scenes of a longhaired hominid's torture and crucifixion. Obviously he was an enemy of some sort.

After another hair-raising cab ride she was back in her cardboard box heating a pot of water on a battery-powered hot plate. She whistled to the tune of a popular television commercial jingle while waiting for the water to boil. Had to borrow the water from a neighbor who erected his corrugated aluminum lean-to around a public drinking fountain, very posh real estate for this part of town, except he had to fight off would-be usurpers and wild dogs on a daily basis to keep his foothold on someone else's property.

Gorb filed a psionic request to scry Annie's complete timeline of memories. Gorb could do stuff like that. The line was busy. Gorb refiled Gorb's request. Access granted. Gorb was given a lifetime pass to Annie's history. Floovia had equipped Gorb with many fantastic powers to accomplish Gorb's mission—literary powers. In addition to telepathy and clairvoyance, Gorb possessed X-ray vision, infrared vision, ultraviolet vision, telescopic vision, microscopic vision, ultrasonic hearing, a canine sense of smell, and the ability to feel what other creatures were feeling. Gorb radiated an aura of indecipherability which effectively made Gorb invisible to most organisms. Gorb could teleport from one location to another, no matter how far apart. Of course the proper forms had to be filed and authorized first.

Although Gorb could read minds, the ability came with one stipulation—Gorb was prohibited from influencing them. Gorb was warned that certain types of minds have the power to influence Gorb when Gorb is reading them. Gorb swore an oath on Brog's hectocotyl tentacle that Gorb would suppress Gorb's Floovian beliefs for the duration of Gorb's visitation here.

Annie's paps handed over the family heirloom on his deathbed. A Victorian syringe of tempered steel, 'twas. She had just turned the mutinous age of thirteen. The 20cc inoculator had been passed down from generation to generation, initially acquired by her great grandpaps who stole it from a doctor's office at the turn of the century. Annie's paps had accidentally pricked himself on the needle and keeled over within ten minutes due to the lethal droplet of pufferfish neurotoxin that leaked from its tip. This unfortunate bungle was bound to happen eventually. Eighteen innocent souls were set free before he finally made the irrevocable error. To his credit, he brought home the bread for a baker's dozen years this way, a long plank to walk for a habitual murderer. Annie's grandpaps had died the same way, and her great grandpaps, too. It had become a family tradition. Annie promptly swiped the needle at the proper moment when the scallywag was too weak to clamp his hands around it anymore, just as he had taught her.

Mams had already dropped out of the family portrait two years prior to go get drunk and do drugs and sleep under freeway overpasses. Paps said it was on account o' she was polar. Little Annie was one tough jibber, raised on a steady program of mental and physical abuse. Severity imparted an infernal wisdom to her. Everyone felt sympathy for poor little orphaned Annie, and she capitalized on it. Paps was sloppy in her opinion, offing people who received regular fortnightly paychecks. People asked questions when certain members of society went missing, especially when those members were employed and useful to someone. Annie lost track of how many times they'd had to pack up their stuff in the middle of the night and move to a different state. The loot never kept them afloat for very long. Paps was always having to supplement his income with petty thefts and robberies. He spent a lot of time in labor camps during Annie's formative years, leaving mams to see the family through with shoplifting and the occasional backstreet tugger. Never a bugger, though. Never a chugger. Annie had a different strategy. Something foolproof. Didn't believe in outright murder. She preferred to paralyze her victims the way a spider does, and let nature run its course while feeding off their comatose husks. Annie had demons in her blood.

At age fourteen she traded three Polaroids of herself in a one-piece swimsuit to a convicted pharmacist in return for alchemical secrets. On the Capricorn morn of her fifteenth birthday she pilfered a pampered fartling's fifth grade chemistry textbook, one of many gifts she gave herself that day. By sixteen the scrofulous little scrog was mixing her own hazardous chemical cocktails using a student laboratory kit she had earned by plying the only trade mams ever taught her, exchanging discreet moments of physical pleasure for predetermined quantities of non-refundable. After many failed experiments (many dead rats later) she developed the perfect concoction to realize her schemes. The ingredients were cheap, and they could be found at any grocery store.

Time moves differently for Gorb. Gorb moves differently through time. Gorb moves through different times. Gorb moves through different Gorbs. Every reader does likewise.

When the water began to froth a boil, Annie turned off the heat and poured in a liberal dose of nail polish remover along with three capfuls of lemon-scented bleach and a sprinkle of nutmeg while stirring. After letting the liquid cool and congeal to the consistency of runny syrup, the old picaroon filled up the family syringe, making sure to rid the mixture of air bubbles. With deviltry grinning across her weatherworn face, she stashed her hypodermic weapon of commerce under the manifold rags comprising her outfit and headed to the same place she'd been going to for the past fifty years, the place no sane person dare enter—the labyrinthine tunnels beneath the city.

The twilight sky was a cat's cradle of power lines. An unsettlingly plenteous number of pigeons were lined up on the crisscrossing wires bombing heads and shoulders and shiny waxed cars in near mint condition parked bumper to tailpipe like tessellated queues of canines greeting one another. Annie had taken the longer route so she could skunker past some of the nicer homes in Middleville, chimneyed sanctums of brick and shingle unperturbed by autumn's frenzied winds or winter wetness. Houses firmly rooted, rife with rooms and windows, most of them dark. They looked empty, but not in an abandoned sort of way. It was like they were models built to full-scale. Occasionally she spied a shadow going about its routine, the glow of a widescreen, a lone cat lazing in the windowsill. Mellow golden porchlights radiated hospitality above every welcoming doormat. Annie suspected the hearts around the hearths weren't nearly as inviting. Hearths she would never feel the warmth of. Beds she could only imagine the comfort of, drizzled in sheets and soft blankets sprinkled with pillows coated in 100% cotton pillowcases that needed frequent laundering, their colors coordinating with plush carpets that needed frequent vacuuming and drapes that needed frequent dusting, and don't forget about the porcelain toilets that needed frequent scrubbing and the linoleum flooring that needed frequent mopping and the dishes that needed frequent washing, lawns that needed frequent mowing and neighbors that needed frequent tending like gardens, not to mention rents that needed paying, on time, every month, along with a pile of other bills necessary to keep the game of civilization going. She passed through the neighborhood as a ghost haunting the streets outside their gabled serenities, rejoicing in her alienation. This was one of the few feelings Gorb could relate to, being something of an extraterrestrial *flâneur*.

Beggars, amputees, and invalids lined the avenue sloping downward to the entrance of the decommissioned subway networks, a dangerous underworld where homeless drifters gathered like cockroaches in the dark. Communities of hobos, winos, crackheads, cutthroats, psychos, schizos, whores, mimes, geets, Elmos and Grovers, Elvis impersonators, and graffiti prodigies devoured one another down below the broken streets of Eden, but nobody ever bothered dear old Annie. Anyone else was fair game. Harassment. Robbery. Severe beatings just for breathing in someone's space, taking up their musty air. Stabbings more customary than handshakes. But not when it came to kindhearted old Annie. Every downtrodden rapscallion secretly prayed that she would come to aid them in their direst hour.

Lighting her way with a stout candle set in a brass candlestick, Annie feigned naive innocence as she hobbled glory-eyed through the sunken city of Hades, smurgling past the usual hooligans and vagrants, all the familiar faces of infamy. Sometimes the faces in the flickering candlelight would be wearing different bodies. Regardless of whoever came and went, their faces always looked the same. The concrete tubes descended three levels deep into crumbling black mazes even the ballsiest underworlders avoided. Only the most wretched lunatics lurked in these subterranean hiding places, abandoned by their brethren. Annie called it the geet market.

In a remote corner of nowhere, she spied a lone sot singing drunkenly to himself:

"Speak softly to yer li'l boy,
Don't beat him when he sneezes,
So he can thoroughly enjoy
The pepper when he pleases!"

The sotty crooner noticed he had an audience. "Hey li'l wrinkly puss," he slurred, "what're ya doin' down here all by yer lonesome in the bowels o' the beast?"

With a feral shine in her eyes, her skeletal fingers curled around the hilt of her syringe, "Yer 'bout to find out!" It was over before he realized what had happened. Unfortunately she injected a finchspit too much, killing him instantly.

She carkled a jolly ditty shopping for her next victim:

"Speak roughly to yer li'l boy,
And beat him when he sneezes;
He only does it to annoy,
Because he knows it teases."

Rats and roaches skit-scatting underfoot. Million-dollar mile after mile of steel rails laid to rust. How long had she been down here? It was hard to tell by the candle's reduction. A couple of hours, maybe. Gorb rounded it to 16,200,000,000,000 nanoseconds, or four and a half hours. Annie only knew she was getting tuckered. Sore knees, ankles swollen to twice their usual swollenness, toes all achy and tingly and numb. Femurs scraping against sandpaper in her hip sockets, that's what every step felt like.

She came across a couple of plastered oafs sleeping on a mattress of exposed springs cluttered in empty beer cans and yellowed newspaper. Thieving cutthroats they were, deserving of Annie's compassion, but the bulkiness of either of their muscular frameworks would prove too troublesome for her to lug around. She preferred a more aeriferous dotterel. Gorb scanned them for parasites, detecting the presence of lice in their hair, mites in their eyelashes, bedbugs on their skin and clothing, tapeworms in their digestive tracts, whipworms in their feces, ringworm (technically a fungus) on the soles of their feet, and a single hyperlexic holomorphasite infesting both of their brains simultaneously. Death incarnate lurched past the two slumbering drunkards. In this particular case death assumed the guise of granny gum-gums.

Canny Annie faux granny was feeling lightheaded. Gorb could sense that her fluid levels needed replenishing; she was dehydrated. "Dry as a mummy's eye," was how she mentally phrased it. She clocked out for a breather, crouching down in the corner between a wide cement column whose fluted length was fanned with cracks and an abutting charred section of wall tiled in broken linoleum. Couldn't seat herself proper on any of the benches at this platform because their metal slats had all but dissolved away from rust. “Criminy!” she carkled. Her galoshes were ankle-deep in a wormy pile of wolf dung. She had already stepped in two other such piles.

The overwhelming funk of bat guano stung her nostrils. She could almost taste it. Staring at the remnant of a sign scribbled over with graffiti, a sign that must have once stated **PLEASE WATCH YOUR STEP** before the tangle of monikers crowded it to **EASE WATCH YOU**, the boundaries of her mind slowly grew and grew, swelling beyond the confines of her senses, spilling into lightless spaces devoid of memories, vacuous gulfs outdistancing intellect, her crooked old body fading away until she could no longer feel anything but the deep pulse of vast cosmic movements, maddeningly intricate harmonies of electromagnetic oscillation woven into murmurous black whirlpools echoing the primordial thunders of a billion trillion supernovae softly underscored by countless vibrating strings of fundamental expression stretched across eternity . . . and then a mouse nearby went *squeak*, plunging her back to this speck of world. Figured she ought to head back to the shack and try again tomorrow. That meant another day without earnings. Probably didn’t have too many days left in her. She got up and kept going, same as always.

The stench of rot coated this stretch of tenebrous railway. Picked over “meowser skellies” and stray batwings bereft of their steersman were a common sight among the rubble. Had to move quiet, keeping the candlelight low. Wolves couldn’t be too far off. The ones down here were hairless, with mousy red eyes and pale hides tough as shark skin. They prowled the danker tunnels, usually sticking to smaller prey than bipeds like Annie, though it wasn't unheard of for a pack to gang up on some poor shpongled bludger in times when easier critters got scarce.

Gorb veered from the tracks to inspect a nook that was particularly dense with carcasses. While testing a recently killed chiropteran for radiation and lead, Gorb noticed a calciferous anomaly strewn among the litter of rat-bat-cat bones. Clearing aside gutted quarries in various stages of decay, Gorb discovered the skeletal remains of something closer to Annie's species, except it only had a single eye socket centrally located in its skull. Gorb disconnected the head from its spine to get a closer look, causing adjacent frameworks to clatter. Annie thought she heard something, a growl, or a groan, the rattling of bones. "Is that ye, Reaper? It's me, Annie." She told herself it was probably just the ringing in her ears. Unless something had picked up her scent. Paranoia was a sort of wisdom down here. But what if . . . supposing . . . *was something following her?* It felt like something was following her. She could feel it in her gut. Could be the gallstones, though. She turned around. Gorb also turned around, to see what she was looking at. Neither one of them saw anything coming from behind.

Gorb stuffed the curious skull through the blowhole directly below Gorb's one big catlike eye, cramming it down into the first of four abdominal pouches to study at a later date. Gorb went to rejoin Annie on the tracks. The old hobbler looked spooked. "I know yer skuggin' 'round here somewhere," she carkled, glancing back and forth. "Show yerself!" She took a cautious step forward. Nothing terrible happened, so she took another. Upon taking a third step she quickly turned around, only half-expecting to catch an eyeful of something actually stalking her. Annie swore she saw the silhouette of a tentacled beast, just for a fraction of a second before it disappeared. A fraction of a second was long enough to send her hightailing it through the pitch-black tunnel, crushing brittle skellies underfoot and kicking aside squeaky squealers, stirring up a tremendous racket.

Annie's bad knee kept her from getting to full speed. She stumbled along the tracks, tripping over warped railroad ties, almost extinguishing the candle in her haste. Gorb hurried after her, narrowly avoiding collision with the ample cushions of her posterior when she abruptly decided to halt. Two pinpricks of incandescent red, that's what she saw glaring in the dark about thirty feet ahead. Whatever it was, it was standing upright. Annie slowly backed away. It crouched down and began advancing "threaterin'ly" toward her. In the becalmed candlelight the thing's nature became clear. It was a man, bearded and hairy, not a thread of clothing on him, *and he was growling.* Crackhead, dusthead, flakkahead, run-of-the-mill schizo, feral child all grown-up now—Annie couldn't tell which. He had the aspect of a dog or a wolf, something ferociously canine. Annie readied the syringe as he got down on all fours and bounded straight for her. The brute was big, a whole lot more than she could handle. She thought about turning tail and making a run for it, but in her condition she'd be a goner for sure. She steadied herself for the onslaught. Wild-eyed and roaring he came barreling into her, knocking the candlestick and syringe from her grip and pinning her under a maelstrom of jagged teeth and clawing, unclipped nails. Annie groped blindly among the rubble for her needle while struggling to fend off his frenzied attempts at biting her face. She couldn't find the needle, but she did spy an opportunity to land a swift galosh in his giblets. He let out a whimpering yelp, unaware the shadows were listening. Something lunged at him, clamping its jaws around his neck, something born of lightless depths, monstrously large and hairless, with pale skin stretched taut over its protruding ribcage. In the overturned candlestick's dying flicker its appearance was somewhat manlike. Gorb was highly stimulated by these events, taking copious mental notes.

Annie snatched the candlestick as the Stygian wolf busied with her assailant. With the candle's aid she found her courage. There it was, gleaming in the rubble—the family heirloom. She scooped up the syringe and scuttled quick as she could to the subway platform about a quarter mile back. Like their kin, hairless albino wolves were pack hunters. Others couldn't be too far behind.

A baleful howl echoed through the tunnel, followed by several yips. The platform was just up ahead. She'd have to cross over to the south line and head back the direction she came until hitting Mulroney Street Station then climb the defunct escalator up to the second level and take the east line all the way to Chinatown Station where there's a staircase guarded by Elvis impersonators (who'll let a soul pass for the bribe of a candy bar) descending to the third level railway lines, if she wanted to keep hunting for someone to care for. Maybe it was time to call it a day. She glanced around. There weren't any wolves on her trail, at least none that she could see in the candle's myopic illumination. She placed her candlestick on the edge of the platform and clambered up the side, rolling to a standstill sprawled out on the deck of Bleecker Street Station. Struggling to get a decent lungful of air, she gave thanks to her Lord, "Thanks—," *gasp*, "fer—," *wheeze*, "—nothin'!"

"Grrrrr!"

She could barely see it. A murky patch of gray emerging from the darkness. "Always gotta have the last laugh, don't ya?" she muttered, demonstrating how difficult the act of standing up can be if you only have two legs. It hopped up from the tracks onto the platform, snarling and pink-eyed and frothy at the mouth, a metaphor unleashed from its fable. There was nowhere for her to run. Gorb considered filing a psionic request to incapacitate the beast, but Gorb knew the request would be denied. Gorb wasn't allowed to interfere. It didn't matter that Gorb might have already interfered.

"Alright, let's do this," she carkled, taking the edge of her bathrobe and wrapping the thick terrycloth around her forearm.

The naked wolf moved from side to side, sizing up Annie with its bloody bestial eyes and baring its saber canines. She held out the arm padded in terrycloth as though it were a bullfighter's lure. Her other hand was clenched around the hilt. The wolf sprang forward, catching more terrycloth than flesh. Annie stabbed her tempered steel needle into its eye and pressed the plunger. A single yelp and the wolf went limp.

Victory afforded little time to catch her breath or tend to her wounds. The wolf's cohorts would come sniffing around soon enough. It's not like her scent was subtle. Scraped and bloodied she scrambled over the platform and made her way down the south line. Had to make this next poke count. The syringe only had enough juice for one more go.

About 3,600,000,000,000 nanoseconds later she heard something other than tinnitus. Her ears pricked up. It wasn't a wolf. Someone was groaning. Just the right pitch of pain. She followed the call to an ideal patient lying catatonic in a pool of his own vomit. The smell of putrefied frog guts lingered in the air around him. His tongue was warty and greenish, side effects of his geety lifestyle, the lifestyle of a psychedelic toad smoker. Annie snuck over to him and knelt by his side. Setting the candlestick down, she whispered, "The Lord has judged ya to be unworthy, a waste o' good flesh. But yer 'bout to become useful. At least once in yer wayward life, yer gonna do someone a bit o' good." The wrinkled saint unveiled her rusty syringe, implement of her mercy, and gently stuck the needle into his jugular.

The toad junkie kicked his legs and grabbed feebly at the liver-spotted hand driving the needle, the last voluntary movements his body would ever make. Spasms and retching came next. Hard Luck Annie caressed him like she was his own mams while he convulsed, trying to ease his transition from sentient mortal to zombie vegetable. She hated needless suffering.

Annie searched him for valuables, only finding a half-eaten chocolate bar in his pocket. "Ya won't be needin' this anymore," she muttered, taking the candy for herself. "Ain't no reason to feed a black market kabob."

Her choice of moneymaker turned out to be a "limpity geet" in his early twenties with herpes simplex virus 1 and 2, hepatitis A and B, syphilis, and a mild case of scurvy. It should be noted that, in addition to scanning him for impurities, Gorb collected a sample of his stool without permission. Annie estimated the bugger might be able to stay alive for about three weeks on a cup of water a day before his biological plumbing finally clogged with clotted blood. She spit on a corner of her apron and cleaned him up a smidge. “There ya go,” she muttered, lifting his limp body, “all nice and polished.” Misjudged his poundage, finding him a bit heavy for the hefting. He’d be thinner soon enough. Had to accustom herself to the new cumbersome adornment, repositioning her unresponsive partner until discovering the optimal pose for cradling him picturesque in their representation of beggarliness. After choreographing the poses, Hard Luck Annie surfaced from the underground railway with renewed vigor. It was a new day and she had a new meal ticket. Life was good, thought Annie.

Gorb skipped ahead to the end of her file. This isn’t so unfathomable when you consider how time actually spirals backwards and forwards and sideways circling around and around and twisting inside out and looping upside down, rippling everywhere at once and nowhere really. It’s just that your hominid senses are only capable of perceiving information as trickling in the linear direction of entropy, your fragile brain unable to process anything that occurs at faster-than-light speeds.

The unmentionable deed was her hobby and job, her meaning for existence, her breakfast, lunch, and dinner. Hard Luck Annie proceeded this way for twenty-seven more years, until a drunken taxi driver took her life after falling asleep at the wheel. When neighbors scavenged her cardboard house, they found an antique metal syringe among the scant knickknacks she had collected throughout her career.

A free clinic was constructed in Annie's name shortly after her fatal accident. The medical facility was funded through a posthumous contribution left by Annie in her will. She wrote her last will and testament on the back of a cashier's check worth ten million dollars. A mortician discovered the check while he was prepping her for cremation. It was rolled up with three five-dollar bills inside a Ziploc bag lodged in her anus.

An idealized statue of Hard Luck Annie cradling a patient in her bosom was erected in the courtyard to commemorate her charitableness. The sculptor, who wished to remain anonymous, mended her rags, softened the bags under her eyes, smoothed the wrinkles on her forehead and cheeks, defined her chin, detangled her hair, and remembered her nose with less of a cauliflower look. A bronze plaque at the base of the statue stated, "I donated more than I ever begged, and I helped more than I ever hindered."

A MAD TEA PARTY
Professor MANSON
Professor APPLEWHITE
Professor JONES
BG 18

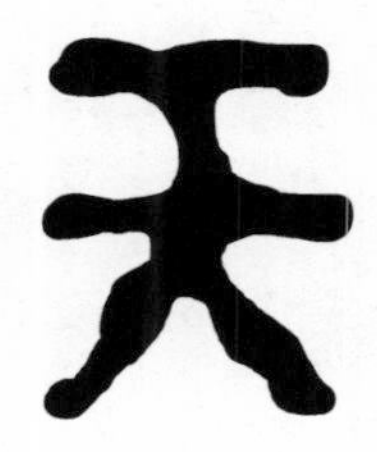

A MAD TEA PARTY

Deeming it superfluous to repeat Annie's cycle, Gorb walked her home and left her to her druthers. Gorb was experiencing technical difficulties. It seemed Annie's homespun dialect was interfering with the settings on the transgrammalexical adaptor. Cogniphonic frequencies were overlapping, yielding inconclusive readouts. Grammatological diagnostics were unreliable. Floovia had equipped Gorb with a test version of the transgrammalexical adaptor, the newest in a long line of prototypes grown specifically for Gorb's mission. The older models could only translate the meaning of words. This was the first model capable of translating the sense of words in context, their feeling. Combined with the innate telepathic ability of Floovia, Gorb was able to experience the psychological worldscapes of Gorb's specimens.

After telepathically consulting the Floovian hive mind, Gorb was instructed to find an expert in the field of contemporary hominid language systems. Gorb scanned the area within a hundred-mile radius to locate the highest verbal IQ, as determined by *Homo sapiens* standards, not Floovian. Gorb pinpointed the likeliest candidate: male hominid, early fifties, two standard eyes, one standard nose, two standard ears, one standard mouth, two standard arms culminating in five standard fingers each, two standard legs culminating in five standard toes each, no visible tail, wearing a brown corduroy blazer with leather patches on the elbows, hurrying off to an appointment of the merrier sort only 3.6 miles away from Gorb's current whereabouts. Gorb filed a psionic request for short-range teleportation.

The lighting of the joint signified their party was underway. Professor Charles Manson, an unfortunate namesake he had learned to live with, skimmed through the pages of a dusty book until he found a specific passage. He had been fascinated with the passage all week. He read it aloud to his guests, "Do you have to tempt a computer mouse with a piece of cheese to discover if it is hungry or not?" He was thin as an ascetic. His eyes bulged wild, haunted by an intelligence desperate to escape the confining dimensions of his brain. The youngest faculty member with tenure, Professor Manson could easily be mistaken for an undergrad. He often looked just as disheveled as the students who attended his early morning lectures, with his uncombed mop of hair and Van Dyke goatee in need of a trim. Professor Manson was the 2010 recipient of the James Joyce *Nebulous Thought* award.

"What kind of question is that?" asked Professor Applewhite, author of seven hundred and eighteen science fiction novels for young adult Christians, six hundred and three steampunk romance novellas, four hundred and forty-six short stories, most of which concern topical issues in Christendom, and one how-to manual on building geodesic birdcages, none of which ever qualified for publication, earning him the dubious distinction of being the most prolific writer never to be published. "It makes my stomach feel queasy. Is this going to turn into another one of your longwinded lectures? I came here to laugh and cry and drink, not especially to think!" He wasn't skinny or fat or strong or weak, his hairline receding into a fine white fuzz. A slender pair of reading spectacles hung from his neck by a sterling silver bead chain.

"The question itself is phrased all wrong," said Professor Jones, whose views were so far beyond postmodernism, postpostmodernism, and postpostpostmodernism that critics often referred to him as a Mostmodernist. "Its wording is dubious. Don't get me wrong, all wording is dubious, but that wording is particularly dubious. The fact that you posed the question here tonight is dubious. The mere act of questioning is dubious. Everything I've just said is dubious." He put the joint to his long flat lips and took a drag, holding it in while he spoke, "Answers are dubious," smoke trickling from his words. "We've never answered a single significant question in our entire lives. Our smartest answers basically amount to explanations for why we don't have answers. We don't really teach history or philosophy or English in the School of Humanities, we teach students how to jam makeshift square pegs into holes that grow infinitely rounder." He rid his lungs of the remaining smoke and took another hit, inhaling and exhaling the acrid particulates casually as breathing. "For instance, if you were to ask me what two plus two equals, you would undoubtedly expect me to say the answer is four.

But let's suppose I have a PhD in four-ology, meaning you'll never get a simple four out of me—I'll tell you there's no such thing as four, or two for that matter, and ask you two of what plus two of what? Two elephants plus two ponies equals something different than two protons plus two electrons. What if one of the elephants is a male and the other is a female? That's very likely to equal something different than two male elephants. Even if there are two male elephants, what if one is very young and the other is very old? That would yield different results than two middle-aged male elephants, especially if we're discussing the price of tusks in China. Are they African elephants or Asian, or one of each? Are there any albinos? Are they in their natural habitat? That certainly affects the equation." He took another puff and blew it out almost immediately. "Ask me what two plus two equals and I'll turn the scenario around and ask you why you're asking such an obvious question. I'll question what your underlying motive is—what's your game, your trap. I'll tell you that two plus two equals two sets of two. I'll tell you that two plus two equals a square if we consider the question geometrically, or a rectangle, possibly a rhombus, even a trapezoid. I'll tell you the answer is equal to seven minus three, or the square root of sixteen. Two aces beats two kings but not four twos. Two inebriated materialists meeting two inebriated idealists in a bar could equal two new drinking buddies. It could just as likely equal a bar brawl. If I'm full of the devil's drink I might even tell you that two plus two equals one memorable night of debauchery, if we're talking about couples who swing that way."

"That's not even close to what we're talking about," said Professor Manson, plucking the joint out of Professor Jones' hand just as he was about to take another drag. “That’s about as far away from what we were discussing as you can get.”

“Oh right, the improperly worded computer mouse problem,” said Professor Jones. “I suppose we could conduct a simple experiment to pinpoint the error, even though nothing can be revealed about the true nature of mice, or anything else for that matter, from observation. Infallible truths aren’t meant for mankind, although I suppose pursuing the pixies is an agreeable way to pass the hours nonetheless.” With a grunt he lifted his bulk from the tufted armchair he had settled into and went to the kitchen to obtain something cheesy . . . cheeselike . . . cheesish . . . grabbing a porous yellow rectangular object from the wooden cutting board on the kitchen counter and then returning to the den. He dangled the porous yellow rectangular object in front of the computer mouse resting on the mouse pad on Professor Manson’s desk. “It seems unresponsive.” He resettled into the tufted armchair. His broad lips and squat body imparted a froggy sort of appearance to him. “Perhaps we should give the query more thought.”

“Introspection only goes so far,” said Professor Applewhite, “before it hits a dead end. Nature instructs us best. Every perspicuous detail of flora and fauna reflects the harmonious wisdom of God’s perfect design. Truth is plain as a farmer tilling the soil, but educated minds tend to make things needlessly complex.” Professor Manson passed him the joint, and he inhaled deeply. He held the smoke in. His ears turned bright red. His impish smile looked ready to burst into laughter at any moment.

"On that note," said Professor Jones, "let's continue this discussion outside. If we're lucky we can compare and contrast the dietary habits of a field mouse with the dietary habits of our computer mouse."

"We don't need to go outside to de-thorn this paw," said Professor Manson, the host of their soiree. "Comparisons between apples and oranges will never solve a watermelon. First we should try to understand the various components involved in the problem." Manson frequently volunteered to host these soirees at his ranch, mainly because he hated going anywhere unfamiliar, like other professors' compounds. His den was designed for carrying on conversations of the profounder sort, paneled in lustrous cherry wood and lined with bookshelves bearing every riddle and enigma of the past five thousand years. Globs of dried goo that were smeared across a framed canvas above the mantel resembled a bearded gentleman in three-quarter view from the waist up, wearing a heavy black coat and peaked captain's cap, staring out from a dark seascape with a faraway look in his eyes.

"Okay, let's start with the cheese," said Jones, licking his pasty lips. His eyes were scribbled red. He inspected the porous yellow rectangular object. "It appears to be cheesoid, of the Swiss variety." He sniffed it. "It's definitely saturated with the odor of fermentation." He took the smallest of bites. "The cheesiness of this cheese is evident to my senses. I'll therefore conclude it's as cheesy as cheese can get, though I'd be remiss not to tell you it's gone a bit stale."

"You've proven nothing!" said Manson. "The cheesiness of cheese cannot be determined through mere sensorial qualities. You must contemplate *yourself*, not the cheese, if you want to understand true cheesiness, the cheesiness from which all cheese arises." He snatched the porous yellow rectangular object away from his colleague and examined it. "Aha! You're getting lax in your old age, Doubting Thomas! The porous property of this sallow cellulose fiber has exposed a glitch in your habit of connecting causes to effects. It seems you've forgotten your Hume."

"You say that like I walked out the door with no pants on," said Jones.

"Your error is just as laughable," said Manson. "Causality is merely a psychological conditioning of expectation arising from the reinforcement of recognized patterns."

"Duh," said Jones.

"Don't *duh* me," said Manson. "You're the one who can't even tell the difference between a piece of Swiss cheese and a moldy yellow dish sponge anymore!"

"Oh no, not my favorite sponge!" blurted Applewhite, coughing up the smoke he'd been holding in this whole time.

"Your favorite sponge?" said Manson. "Whoever heard of such a thing? I bought it at the 99-cent store. It came in a four-pack."

"*It* has a name," said Applewhite. "SpongeySam Sudshorts!"

Manson let out a snort.

"Our beloved Applewhite," said Jones, "saintliest of the serpent's apple seeds. Blessed are the altruists, for they shall inherit the chore of washing the dishes."

"Now if I could just get him to vacuum," said Manson, "the maid could have the day off."

"Don't tease!" said Applewhite. "That sponge was dear to me! Hundreds upon hundreds, no, thousands upon thousands of besmirched dishes received their purification through that blessed sponge!"

"Or one just like it," murmured Manson.

"Alas, what will I ever do without Spongey?" said Applewhite. "The hour of cleansing is nigh!"

"Quit acting so melodramatic," said Manson, tossing the porous yellow rectangular object (which may or may not have been cheese depending on which professor you asked) to the sentimentalist. "Most of it is still there."

Gorb calculated that 97.32% of the original specimen remained.

"If SpongeySam cannot exist in his undamaged entirety, then he shan't exist at all!" shouted Applewhite, and he stuffed the porous yellow rectangular object into his mouth and swallowed it in a single gulp, with some difficulty.

"It must have been a piece of cheese," said Jones. "No sane person would eat a sponge."

"Unless they mistook it for a chunk of stale Swiss," said Manson. He picked up an open bottle of merlot waiting for him on the end table and hastened to the burnished leather sofa where Professor Applewhite was struggling with his swallow. The wine was pressed by Charles Shaw, sold at Trader Joe's, and pilfered by Manson from yesterday's faculty meeting. "Well, what was it?" said Manson, refilling Applewhite's empty glass and prompting him to take a drink. "A sponge or a piece of cheese? Speak up, impetuous spirit!"

Gorb could have easily determined the molecular composition of the object in question, but Gorb had not traversed the infinite infinities of hyperspace to come here and determine the truth or untruth of their cheese. Gorb was here to translate and transmit the subjective experience of their confusion.

Applewhite took a drink to lubricate his throat. He took another to lubricate his mind. "I'm too distressed to think about it right now." He sighed. "Give me a few minutes to compose myself."

"Look here you ham, I'm not asking for much," said Manson, getting a bit annoyed. "Just tell that spiked Kool-Aid sipping sot of a despot he's got everything wrong from Apriori to Zarathustra!"

"You must be jesting!" said Jones. "You wouldn't have been able to write your *Critique of Fallacious Reasoning* if I hadn't written *An Enquiry Concerning Human Irrationality*. Your entire confounding treatise could be interpreted as a direct response to mine."

Professor Manson replied, "Someone had to point out your errors."

Professor Jones' cheeks turned ruddy. He was noticeably peeved, and the fact that he was noticeably peeved only inspired Manson to peeve him more, "Honestly, what branch of logic casts doubt upon the logical method from which it is derived? Why not just saw off your feet while you're at it?"

Professor Jones exploded, "A rigorous logician cannot blindly adhere to the methodologies of logic! All our lives follow from the premise that *A* is not *B*, or *B* is not equal to *A*. It seems obvious enough, right? Wrong! Open that myopic third eye of yours! All of our problems stem from the presupposition that *A* is not *B*! This is the fundamental equation of difference, of othering—the foundation of desire! It's the equation of appearances—symbols that journeyed so far from home they forgot their way back. *B* is not equal to *A* encourages prejudice and lazy reasoning. The well-rounded intellect must also consider the contrary—that *A* is *B*, and *B* is indeed equal to *A*! *A* is not *B* simply answers the question *what is? B* is equal to *A* forces one to ponder *how so?* They're both linear symbols, for one thing, and they both have Greek ancestry. *A* and *B* bleed equally from the same pen. They're both printed in black ink against the white backdrop of every page in your library. If you really think about it, *A* contains *B*. *A* is only *A* by virtue of *B*'s existence. *B* is inherent in *A*, along with every other letter representing the range of human sounds. The vibrations of *A* and *B* issue equally from the same vocal source."

"Try plotting your course on a map with *A* equals *B*," said Manson, "or spelling the word *baby*."

"There you go again, playing obtuse. You know precisely what my point is. *A* is not *B* puts a stopper on thought. *B* is equal to *A* invites you to exercise your imagination. *A* equals *B* fosters empathy. It asks you to get inside the symbols and do some exploring, or rather, it conditions you to see beyond the facade of their duality."

"Then why not ask your students to fill out their next Scantron form with the proviso that *A* equals *B*?" said Manson.

Floop! Floop! An alarm went off inside Gorb's empathic analyzer. Gorb was beginning to take a side in the argument. Gorb decreased the sensory intake to 33%.

"The critics were astute in their assessment of your latest project," said Jones. "Jelinko, Pittman, Strausselberg, myself—our reviews were largely similar: Magnum opus? More like minimum opus! You've philosophized yourself into the role of an unknowably impenetrable object!"

Professor Manson gasped. “You take that back! The critics are never right! I am not unknowably impenetrable, nor am I an object! I’m only the *appearance* of an unknowably impenetrable object! I stated it plainly at the bottom of page two hundred and eighty-eight in section D of the fourteenth footnote! And I quote, ‘Beyond the fugacious shell of stimuli that every not-me perceives me to be, I am the somatic crystallization of transcendental apperception, the architect of time and space, a whirlwind of words and objects and events coalescing into the subconscious. I am the soul of this nation, the expression of this world. Limitless and ever-changing, I am the potential for every experience humanly possible!’”

“You’re both objects,” interrupted Applewhite, “of my desire! Gosh I love playing charades in Plato’s cave with you fellows!” He raised his wineglass for a toast, “To your health, brothers!” and drained its crimson entirety. Gorb scanned the medical records in their DNA databases. All three were suffering from ailments that would soon claim their lives. Jones was dying of stomach cancer, pleurisy was snuffing out Applewhite’s terrestrial flame, and Manson was an asthmatic hypochondriac. Sickliness was the norm for him, but his condition had gotten much worse lately.

Professor Applewhite continued to gush, “Truly and sincerely I mean every honeyed word that drips from my poesy of tongue and paeanic lips when I swear that no dearer friends were ever befriended in the entire history of friendship!”

“Really?” said Manson in his slithery way. “That’s strange,” baring his fillings and bridges and crowns, “because we can barely tolerate your ostentatious outpourings of drivel.”

"Phooey to your teasing," said Applewhite. "Sarcasm is the basest example of wit. Despite your thorny demeanor, I know your love for me doth rival my love of thee."

"How exactly do you know that he reciprocates your love, as *thou sayest*?" said Jones.

"I can't explain it, dearest chum. I just feel it to be true, and that's enough for me."

"Then you don't really know anything, do you, old boy?" said Jones. "You merely have faith in your beliefs."

Professor Applewhite frowned. "Piffle! I know plenty. For instance, I know you don't believe in God, and the faithless aren't fit to talk about faith."

"Preposterous!" said Jones. "Reason is capable of comprehending faith. The difference between belief and fantasy teeters on the degree of emotion one invests in a concept, determined by one's personal experience."

"What a dead way of putting it," said Applewhite, pouring the rest of the bottle into his glass. "Your words have just murdered the spirit of faith."

Professor Jones felt an obsessive need to explain himself, which meant persuading others to agree with him. Gorb found this behavior odd considering the professor's general lack of respect for everyone else's intellect. "Everyone is a propagandist," he said. "To put it differently, every one of us is a reflection of our favorite brands of propaganda. We can't help but regurgitate our beliefs anytime we express ourselves."

"If I wanted to listen to a sermon, I'd preach one of my own," said Applewhite. "I can pound a pulpit with the best of them!" He hiccupped, looking a bit wobbly from the buzz. Hiccupping a second time, he took a swig of merlot to wash down the porous yellow wad lodged in his esophagus. "By the way, did we ever figure out if that sponge was a piece of cheese or not?"

"Don't concern yourself with it," said Manson. "It's not important anymore."

"What's that you say?" said Jones. "What's not important anymore?"

"Everything," said Manson. "It doesn't matter what any of us has to say. It's all been said before."

"Then why should anyone bother to say anything?" said Applewhite.

"Tut-tut, old boy," said Jones. "We have to earn a living somehow, don't we?"

"What's wrong with you, Jim?" said Applewhite.

"I nurture my pain like it's a newborn puppy," said Jones.

"More like it's Ebola Zaire," added Manson.

Professor Jones took the last possible hit off the sticky remains of the joint and then mashed it into a ceramic ashtray shaped like a heart, where it smoldered. "Are you saying I shouldn't get close to anyone?"

"Not at all," said Manson. "Go out there and infect as many puppies as possible."

Miss Brunner entered the room carrying a silver tray loaded with an array of brightly colored objects cut into various geometric shapes which appeared to be edible because similar objects had proven themselves edible in past experiences. It was unlikely they were sponges. Sponges and cheese tasted the same to Gorb. So did granite and fire. Gorb could detect chemical differences in the molecular composition of a substance, but Gorb lacked the ability to taste flavors in the hominid sense. Gorb was not equipped with taste buds. The detection of sodium chloride indicated salt, but there was no attendant saltiness. Sucrose indicated the substance was sugary, but there was no sweetness. Miss Brunner was Professor Manson's personal assistant, although scanning her body hinted at something more. Gorb found Manson's fingerprints on her. Gorb also detected Manson's unborn son growing in her, roughly the size of a raindrop. "Pardon me, sirs. I overheard part of your earlier conversation, and thought perhaps it would be wise to rephrase that mousy question in clearer terms."

"Brilliant idea, Linda Dee!" said Manson. He reread the question aloud and then spent a moment pondering its deeper significance. "I think I've got it." He stated his revision triumphantly, "If reason is the act of using experience to infer effects from causes, does knowledge rely solely on interaction?"

"No, no, no, you completely missed the target as usual," said Jones, and he offered his own version, "The question is asking if there are any intuitive modes of understanding that function independently from experience."

Miss Brunner cleared her throat. "Pardon my interruption, but I believe you gentlemen just said the same thing."

Professor Manson looked crossly at his assistant, "Thank you for the observation, Linda Dee. That will be all for this evening. Goodnight."

"Sorry, professor."

"I said *goodnight*."

"Now it's Marshall's turn to restate the question," said Jones.

As the two professors stared at him, Applewhite massaged his forehead contemplatively. He paused to take a sip from his wineglass, then resumed his intellectual chore. Minutes dragged.

"You're taking too long," said Manson.

Professor Applewhite found his colleague's impatience amusing. "Too long for whom?" swirling the wine in his glass and taking another sip. "The world moves too fast for my liking nowadays. Too many people view life as a busy blur flashing by from the confines of their motorcar. I simply refuse to live like that. Where is everybody in such a hurry to go? Racing to their graves, that's where. Will any of our sandcastles still be standing in a thousand years? How about a million? The starry firmament takes longer than that just to pass gas." He leaned to one side and let out fifty-three decibels of flatulence, presumably for effect. "Leave the clockwork to the cuckoos. I'm going to park along the side of the road and enjoy a leisurely picnic of sour grapes and humble pie any time I happen to spy an idyllic stretch of grass."

Professor Jones looked puzzled. "Motorcar? Firmament? How delightfully antiquated."

Professor Applewhite continued, "So what's important to me, you might venture to ask, even though you never do, and I might say, oh, I don't know, how are you? Are you okay? Is there anything I can do? I might hug you, or kiss you, maybe buy you a drink, or simply hold your hand and listen to you, and love you, the ugly you, the misrepresented you, the misled you, the delusional you. So many bodies, so little love. No shortage of lust, though."

"Sentimental rubes like you fall in love every day," said Jones. "You're in love with love itself. It's not about the person. It's not even about the orgasm. It's about the neurochemicals, isn't it? You're addicted to the emotional high."

"He still hasn't reformulated the question," said Manson.

"What's with all this hamster-wheeling anyhow?" said Applewhite. "The question is what it is, and it means whatever you want."

Professor Jones' usual look of condescension turned to one of surprise. "That was surprisingly apropos, Marshall."

"A keen insight," affirmed Manson.

Professor Applewhite chuckled. "I wholeheartedly agree, though I have no idea what it meant."

Professors Manson and Jones exchanged knowing glances.

"Let's quit this maddening hide-and-go-seek game of truth," said Applewhite. "It's not fun anymore. Uncork another bottle of the transubstantial blood of our merciful savior and I'll tell you what one my students tried to pull last semester, a frat boy of course, like I'm supposed to care about his academic probation even though he doesn't care enough to earn a passing grade, you know the type, five minutes late to every class, has an implausible excuse for everything, spends more time stalking you online than actually studying for his exams, turns in slapdash essays Monday after the Friday due date but flies off the handle if you take longer than ten minutes to respond to his email asking about extra credit, parents threatening to sue the school . . ."

And so the topic veered, lost in a Bermuda Triangle of their own creation. Gorb had recently visited the Bermuda Triangle. Gorb entered this pocket of the omniverse through the Bermuda Triangle, known to Floovians as Gate #Δ. The trio talked about everything and nothing, playing at games of logomachy until, in the words of Applewhite, "Helios chased Selene beyond the horizon." Their original question was never answered. Gorb was baffled by their wasteful expenditure of words. According to Wikifloovia, "The goal of carbon-based language systems is to exchange information as clearly and persuasively as possible in order to structure the ultraverse in the image of the speaker's preferred form of ignorance. 99.99999997% of the carbon-based systems of information in Sector Octogintillion-C42B of Hyperquadrant Septuagintacentillion-K23H are psychosociobiologically motivated to edit or delete uninformative, redundant, irrelevant, inaccurate, ambiguous, or superfluous communicative transmissions, with deviations occurring primarily for aesthetic purposes. The U.S. American strain of English in particular is noted for its efficiency and pragmatic sensibility, its emphasis on utility, having evolved to reflect the ideals of its symbionts." Gorb would have to edit the outdated passage later.

"Reeowr," said Professor Manson's black cat, staring up at Gorb. Any organism that was completely willing to suspend judgment could perceive Gorb on a rudimentary level. Gorb filed a psionic request to link with the feline's mind. The request was approved without delay. The black cat's caregiver had named it Ninja, but in feline its name was Hwongzong. It felt safe to be Hwongzong. To be an indoor cat. Protected by a giant godly thing. A giant godly thing that took care of its environment, cleaning its wastes, feeding it, making sure it had clean water to drink, looking out for its welfare. Loved by a giant godly thing that responded to its needs. The feeling was warm and vibratory, slightly ticklish.

Gorb noticed something else rotating in Hwongzong's mind. Something very subtle, long repressed. A longing to get out of the house and bask in the sunshine. To chase a mouse. To taste blood.

"Whoa! You smell different," is what Hwongzong had said initially. "Who are you?"

"Gorb is Gorb," said Gorb telepathically, speaking feline.

"Reeowr," said Hwongzong, which translated to, "What are you doing here?"

"Gorb's primary function is to decipher and transmit the experience of comprehending the ultraverse through primitive alien signification systems, in this case the verbal economy of twenty-eight officially recognized U.S. American dialects and subdialects of the English linguiverse, a linguiverse which currently comprises over four hundred million distinct worlds evolved from a fusion of Classical Greek, Latin, Germanic, Old Norse, and Norman French forebears with mathematical appropriations from Greek, Chinese, Indian, Arabic, and Roman sources."

"Mreeow," said Hwongzong, which meant, "Do you have anything to eat?"

Gorb bent down and stroked Hwongzong from his triangular ears to the tip of his tail, vacuuming off twenty-three fleas to be studied at a later date, after which Gorb froze Hwongzong with a temporal stasis ray and stuffed him in Gorb's third abdominal pouch, to be studied at a later date. (Gorb should have been more careful. Gorb should have filed a request for acquisition before collecting any live specimens. The professors were a bad influence, befuddling Gorb with their compromised linguiversal states. Gorb had never been so drunk or high on language before. Gorb had caught a slight buzz off Annie's cant, but the impairment was nothing compared to this. It seemed this latest version of the transgrammalexical adaptor worked a little too well. Gorb had an alarming thought—if Gorb was intoxicated, was all of Floovia likewise intoxicated?)

Professor Applewhite leaned forward on the sofa. He put on his spectacles, then adjusted them, then tilted them up and leaned forward even further, squinting as though he were trying to figure out what he was seeing. "Do you fellows see that?" he said, pointing toward the bookcase, where Professor Manson's black cat appeared to be hovering about three feet above the floor, floating there stiff as a snapshot, defying their eyes, affronting their minds. And then the black cat vanished, swallowed up by an invisible presence, leaving three distinguished professors twitching on the floor with their eyes rolled back to the whites.

THE QUEEN'S CROQUET GROUND
MRS. MASON
BG
18

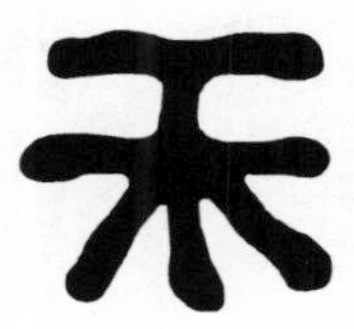

THE QUEEN'S CROQUET GROUND

The doorbell ding-donged. Doorbells only know how to say, "Someone is pressing me." The mailman had arrived with a package. He rang the doorbell again. Intoxicated on words soaked in wine, Gorb left the rhetoricians behind to spend some time sobering up in the mailman's mind. Along his route the mailman chanced upon a black and white mime, a battered Jain at the scene of a crime, an old beggar begging blind, a prostitute he had recently maligned, and peeking through the venetian blinds, a naked Mrs. Rhoyd and Mr. Hiemann entwined in rhythmical grind. The mailman's eyes gorged on everything he saw, reducing the world to rinds and picked over carcasses. His skeptical ears belittled everything he heard, his cynical mouth putrefied everything he said. He threw away Mr. Baker's mail because Mrs. Baker had once looked at him funny in passing. He threw away Mr. Butcherson's mail because Mr. Butcherson had once lodged a complaint to the post office about not receiving a time-sensitive document in a timely manner. He threw away

Mr. Cleaver's mail just because he could. He's thrown away checks and final notices, kept Valentine's packages for himself. Christmas presents, too. He's peed on parcels, stuck envelopes in the crevice between his butt cheeks, and generally befouled deliveries with snot and spittle and armpit sweat, rough handling, dog droppings, bird droppings, whatever was available. He had killed a man in Reno just to watch him die. He was the egg man. He was the walrus. Or were those just song lyrics in his head? The transgrammalexical adaptor was still behaving rather peculiar.

After fifty-seven catcalls, eighty-three putdowns, three hundred and sixty-two furtive acts of disrespect, and one slap in the face, the mailman came to 408 East Civic Center Drive. The dwelling oozed like an infected sore with ectoplasm, psychoplasm, orgoplasm, metaplasm, and three other unidentifiable interdimensional residues. Gorb disconnected from the mailman's mind, feeling somewhat more lucid. Gorb increased Gorb's telepathic capacity to Immersion Level Floox without filing a psionic request, fully aware that Floovia would never approve such a request, and raised the transgrammalexical adaptor's empathy setting to 78%. Sensing it was unsafe to enter the contaminated area, Gorb waited patiently in the driveway to see what would emerge. The day passed into night. The night passed back into day. At 10:16 AM the front door opened five centimeters, just enough for something to peek out.

Mrs. Mason wore a smile. It wasn't a happy smile, or an amused smile, or a sly smile, or even a condescending smile. It was the smile before the downfall, the smile of inescapable horror, of terror given unbridled reign, of great tribulation. Of confusion masked, of chaos feigned tame. A smile disconnected from the lips and chin and cheeks which formed its subtle contour. A smile divided from smiling. A smile longing to smile. The performed smile. The trained smile. The ruse of a smile. Thin lips thinner seen without lipstick, tightly sealed, reserving teeth brushed and flossed and worn to fractured nubs from gnashing. Mrs. Mason suffered a smile. She was the chosen messenger of God, and not just any God—the One True God.

The house named 408 East Civic Center Drive was something other than a home. Mrs. Mason stood in the doorway, eyeing the world like a stranger. The immigrants so brown and glistening under the midmorning summer blaze, their blades deadly sharpened for shearing clipping pruning. *Better slaves than thieves,* thought Mrs. Mason, inspecting the laborers in her front yard, her laborers, wondering what the three of them were conspiring. "Those ones aren't ripe yet, Juan."

"Oh gracias, *Meeesus* Mason," said Jose, accustomed to being addressed as Juan whenever Mrs. Mason was around. Gorb was 99.98% certain that his elongation of her prefix was an act of disrespect. "¡Pinche gringa! La revolución no es una manzana que se cae cuando está listo. Lo tiene que hacer caerse."

"Don't overwater them, Carlos."

"Oh yo nunca, *Meeesus* Mason," said Juan, accustomed to being addressed as Carlos whenever Mrs. Mason was around. "¡Vieja cabra! Una revolución es una lucha a muerte entre el futuro y el pasado."

"You there, I can't seem to recall your name—put your shirt back on. It's indecent, strutting around out here half-naked."

"Oh lo siento, *Meeesus* Mason," said Carlos, accustomed to being addressed as "Hey You" or "You There" whenever Mrs. Mason was around. "¡Típica de Estados Unidos, los hipócritas! Se equivocan pura ilusión de realidad, la licencia para la libertad, la traición por patriotismo, y la venganza por justicia."

Her work here done, she locked the door, then checked the door to prove it was locked, then checked it again just to make sure, and off she flitted. Savages, taught and tamed, but not too much.

The sunny day was a ruse of the devil. Premature onslaughts of pearly gray streaked through Mrs. Mason's brunette perm, complemented by her finest faux pearl necklace, sans makeup, sans nail polish, modesty down to the undergarments. Quiet hundred-year-old houses tapered to thirty-year-old apartment complexes leaking noisome children everywhere that gave way to ten-year-old stacks of office cubicles coated in concrete along Mrs. Mason's path. She had a foot patrolman's march, leaning slightly forward with her hands clasped behind her back, eyes facing downward to avoid the stare of people passing by—sinful miracles walking alone and in pairs, their shadows stretching like musical notes across the paved stave of sidewalk playing out the tragic song that was their life. They were all on the verge of becoming corpses. Mrs. Mason was obsessed with this thought.

"Copper for a lopper, queenie?" begged a bum, obstructing the sidewalk with his siesta, reposed on the pavement with his legs crossed, hands folded casually behind his head in lieu of a pillow, a black bowler hat tilted over his eyes to block out the harsh sunlight. He was dressed in a baggy red plaid suit and matching bowtie, a daisy tucked in the breast pocket, big yellow patches on his elbows and knees. His shoes were size twenty-six extra-extra-extra wide. His nose was red and bulbous, his face painted stark white with an exaggerated smile. The green and white polka-dotted handkerchief hanging from his pocket was the length of a bedsheet. The avenue to Mother Mary's was lined with these characters, and they were especially aggressive on Sundays. A gauntlet of round red noses and painted happy faces. Pink cotton candy goatees. Balloon switchblades.

Gorb wasn't feeling very Gorb. Gorb was on the fritz. Gorb's telepathic connection was experiencing static. The transgrammalexical adaptor wasn't working properly either—the absurdity filter was only functioning at a tenth of its normal capacity, and the irony detector wasn't registering anything, even though irony was impossible to avoid in this sector of the linguiverse. Mrs. Mason was somehow interfering with Gorb's reception.

"Ay, my queen! Without a rich heart, wealth is an ugly beggar," said an ugly beggar in checkered harlequin rags.

"Anyone can quote a quote," said Mrs. Mason.

"Damn near impossible not to nowadays!" said Hard Luck Annie, cradling her care on the street corner, a youth with vacant eyes and a greenish tongue covered in warts. She sang a little tune for the benefit of Mrs. Mason:

"Life is so much shorter,
Shorter than ya know,
So chug yer beer and love with cheer,
'Fore shovin' off ya go!"

However, Mrs. Mason had a tune of her own:

"Life is so much longer,
Longer than you know,
So say your prayers and pay your fares,
Lest Judgment lay you low!"

Annie felt genuine pity for Mrs. Mason. "Best o' luck, deary."

Mrs. Mason felt genuine pity for Annie. "God bless you, dear soul."

The queue to the confessional stretched out the cathedral doors and around the corner. Mrs. Mason could stand in line for twenty minutes or she could get a seat near the altar. She sided with her sore feet.

Everyone was garbed in their Sunday finest at Mother Mary's, that is, everyone except for Sara Butcherson, who, in Mrs. Mason's opinion, was *blossoming into a little jezebel, but thou shalt not judge, lest thee be judged, though I would never let my daughter wear something like that to the House of God almighty, something so sinful, Beelzebub threads woven by the talons of Moloch himself. What in God's name was Ruth Butcherson thinking, letting her daughter shame herself and her family and the Holy Roman Catholic Church and all of Christendom by wearing a skirt that shows off her bare knees? Honestly, if Sam Butcherson were a better father—a better Christian—he would forbid the devil to enter his household, he would forbid his children to dress like whoremongers and harlots, he would forbid his wife to wear so much makeup, he would forbid his eyes to linger so intently on Mrs. Rhoyd's double-D deviltry, but judge not, for God Himself will surely judge that entire family of two-faced hypocrites to eternal damnation and hellfire when the Day of Reckoning comes.*

Father Antipadrosa shimmied down the aisle robed in the most glorious gown to grace the cathedral, his half-meter miter and white silk stole bejeweled in rhinestones and sequins and silver bells braced with gold filigree, his processional tail hymning ancient Babel, *"Everywhere I go, your face I see. Every step I take, you take with me. Nowhere to run to baby, nowhere to hide . . ."* bearing the righteous regalia appropriate to our holiest of holies: waxen wicks to burn, the Holy Word made flesh leather-bound and typographically transfigured into Times New Roman, myrrh billowing from an ornate brass censer. *"Phew!"* blurted Mrs. Mason, *curse that stinky hippy stuff! Honestly, what kind of gift is that for our Lord? Frankincense and myrrh? Why not just give Him a pack of cigarettes? Smoke is smoke, after all. Oh, His precious little Holy Lungs! It seems two of the three wise men weren't so wise, but still, let him who is without sin cast the first stone, though it would've never crossed my mind to get such an inconsiderate gift for my child, or anyone else's. It's practically criminal.*

"Let's all give a shout out to the Father, the Son, and the Holy Spirit!" said Father Antipadrosa. "Can I get an amen?" putting a cupped hand to his ear.

"Amen!" shouted his audience, also called his flock, a term that could refer to an assembly of sheep or birds. Gorb had studied the avian descendants of *Archaeopteryx lithographica* upon arriving here. The last time Gorb was here, there were no birds. Only saurians, big ones. Gorb was eaten twice. Gorb had observed a community of sparrows for five days, dissecting three male specimens and two female, one of which was twelve hours away from laying eggs. Birds were the only vertebrates on this planet possessing feathers and fused collarbones, commonly referred to as wishbones. Contrary to lore dating back over two thousand years, breaking the wishbone had no discernible effect on quantum dynamic processes. After sparrows came chickens. Gorb studied a single hen for three days. Contrary to popular belief, chicken tasted nothing like *Homo sapiens*. There were nineteen billion chickens enslaved on this planet at the time of Gorb's visitation, outnumbering *Homo sapiens* by almost three to one. If their cognitive capacity were increased by 12.85%, they would most likely overthrow their captors.

"Good Gawd! Now that's what I'm talking about! Grace and peace be with you, brothers and sisters!"

"Same to you, Daddy-O," said his flock in unison. A congregation of crows is said to form a murder. Flamingos form a flamboyance, owls form a parliament, swans form a ballet, and ducks in a pond are a paddling. Gorb had observed a community of ducks for seven days. Ducks possessed built-in navigation systems incorporating the planet's magnetic field—granules of magnetite, embedded just above their nostrils. They were intelligent enough to know that flying together in V-formations would reduce friction on their wings, enabling them to cover more distance while expending less energy. They also knew how to use the sun as a compass, and even memorized the position of constellations relative to the North Star. Ducks possessed more useful knowledge than most *Homo sapiens*.

"All right, now sit your fannies down so we can get on with this shindig," said Father Antipadrosa, pulling out his sacred little aspergillum and giving it a dip in the old aspersorium, sprinkling the congregation with droplets of divinity. "That's right! Come on, brothers and sisters! Let the Holy Spirit flood over you! All over your face! All over your body! Bathe in it! Put it in your mouth! Taste it! Good Gawd! Come upon thee, oh Lord! Sweet Jesus, enter into us! Let us be likened unto this blessed water—formless, transparent, and ultimately corrosive! Hallelujah!"

"Hallelujah!" echoed his flock. Gorb knew from experience that a duck's quack echoes too, contrary to urban legend. Ducks were one of the few species of birds equipped with penises. Their penises were shaped like corkscrews, with erections averaging twenty centimeters in length, based on Gorb's measurement of ten specimens. A local database claimed their penises regrew to different lengths on a yearly basis. Gorb could not diverge from Gorb's mission long enough to personally confirm this. Their penises functioned by springing forward and ejaculating in less than half a second. Gorb correlated this stabbing movement with the aggressive mating habits exhibited by the males of the species. It was not uncommon for two or more male ducks to gang up on a lone female and force copulation. Female ducks had learned to fool their assailants with dead-end pockets lining their vaginas, having no legal recourse in the society Anatidae.

Mrs. Mason bowed her head and closed her eyes and clasped her hands, praying fiercely. *Lord, have mercy. Christ, have mercy. Ease my suffering. Ease my heavy burden. All food turns to bitter ashes in my mouth. All I smell is rot, and all I see are corpses. All my words fall dead to the barren soil of this world. Set me free. Please, set me free. Take me now. Don't put me through this anymore. Not another day. I can't do it. Please, I'm ready. Set me free. Father, have mercy. Father, please forgive me. Daddy. Forgive me. I'm sorry for whatever I've done. I'm sorry for everything. I wasn't good enough. I know that now. I took them for granted. I didn't deserve them. I'm sorry. I'm sorry. I'm sorry . . .*

"Amen!" said Father Antipadrosa.

"Amen!" responded the flock, and the choir burst into song, "*Baby, everything is alright, uptight, outta sight . . .*" with the whole congregation back up on their feet, clapping their hands, grooving to the rhythm. Except for Mrs. Mason. She alone remained seated with her head bowed, sobbing.

At the hymnbook's closing the congregation took their seats once more. *"Whew!"* said Father Antipadrosa, "Brothers and sisters, take a couple minutes to pray in silence while I catch my breath," but Mrs. Mason was already praying, clasping her hands so tight her fingers were turning purple, eyes closed to the world outside, screaming with her inner voice to block out every other sound, *please Father, reveal Yourself unto me, for I am Your humble servant, I am Your vessel, I am the cross in which to drive Your nail, I am the flesh upon which to test Your flail, I am nothing without You in my life, mere dog spit, even lower, worm dung, slimy worm dung, so reveal Yourself unto me, oh Lord of all creation, heavenly Father, show Your true Face, most mysterious of all mysteries, most glorious of all glories, highest of all highs, for I am Your humblest servant, Your most loyal follower, Your biggest fan, please Father, I implore You, reveal Yourself unto me, right here, right now, in whatever miraculous manner You deem—burning bush, pillar of fire, ray of white light, spotless dove, talking donkey, I'm not choosy*, and when she opened her eyes, there was Gorb hovering right in front of her, focusing on her with Gorb's one big catlike eye.

"Are you an angel?" said Mrs. Mason, staring up in awe. The congregants seated near her noticed she was talking to herself.

"Gorb is Gorb," said Gorb, speaking telepathically.

"Please, tell me what heaven is like," said Mrs. Mason, clasping her hands pleadingly, voice crackling with aged desperation. Ruth Butcherson glanced over at her and rolled her eyes. John Hiemann scooted an additional six centimeters away from having to sit beside her.

"Heaven is an impractical version of Floovia."

"What is God like?"

"God is an impractical version of Floovia."

"I don't understand," said Mrs. Mason, eyes glossy with welling tears.

"Shhh!" said Edgar Rhoyd from the pew behind. Sara Butcherson was smirking at her.

Mrs. Mason had barely turned her eyes away from Gorb for two seconds, but when she looked for Gorb again, Gorb was gone, even though Gorb was still hovering in front of her, focusing on her with Gorb's one big catlike eye.

"Brothers and sisters," said Father Antipadrosa, "we are gathered here today to contemplate our Lord's suffering, His anguish, His torment on the cross. We are gathered here today to contemplate *The Passion of the Christ*," and he cued the altar boy to start up the film by Mel Gibson, an edited version due to time constraints, two hours pared down to thirty minutes of graphic violence shown larger than life across a widescreen monitor above the pulpit. *Oh poo*, thought Mrs. Mason, *I've seen this a hundred times*. Gorb knew this was untrue. The actual number was much higher. She had seen the movie every Sunday for the past five or six years, maybe longer. It was difficult for Gorb to determine exact historical details concerning Mrs. Mason. Her memories were murky. Deliberately so, as if she were hiding things from herself. Swimming through the psychoplasm of her mind, Gorb had to keep switching the filters and refocusing the lens of Gorb's one big catlike eye in an effort to read whatever glimmers of memory were legible. Church wasn't always this way. Every Sunday used to feel like Christmas, before sin became believable. When hope was still intact. When pride could be put to death by the Word and reborn as faith through the Blood of her Savior in an hour flat. Before her first blood arrived. Before the flood. She tried going to one of those mega-churches. Too anonymous. She tried going to a smaller parish. Too intimate. There was just enough sin at Mother Mary's for her liking. *If it's written, produced, and directed by Mel Gibson, does that mean he's cast himself in the role of God? The film is just so violent, certainly not appropriate for decent God-fearing Christians . . . oh Lordy, that was a doozy of a daydream. I hope angels don't actually look like that. It's always wise to test the spirits. The devil's minions would love nothing more than to drag my immortal soul down to their sulfurous pit, there to claw the flesh off my face and bite off my tongue and pluck out my eyes and rip at my breasts and rape me repeatedly with pitchforks while stroking their thick serpentine erections and ejaculating red hot lava all over my naked body . . .*

"Pay attention to this next part," said Father Antipadrosa, "don't you dare avert your gaze from the gore! I want you to feel it! I mean *really feel it!* Experience it! He did all this for *your* sins! Hallelujah!"

"Hallelujah!" parroted his flock, as the man on the screen was chained and choked and beaten and whipped and flogged and stabbed and spit upon and . . .

Mrs. Mason was staring at twelve ivory roses adorning the altar. The pale roses were indistinguishable in appearance from nature's template, except these would never die. *A rose is a rose is a petunia, pretty little things, how sad that they have to go away so soon, how sad indeed, and where do they go, they're alive too, it's all alive, and all is God, praise the Lord, everywhere I look, God, every thought I have, God, everything that ever happens to me, God, the pretty little petunias, God, but I am not God, that would be sacrilege, and the devil is certainly not God, though he's from God, but then where did my angina come from, and my arthritis, surely not from our heavenly Father, which can only mean one thing—the devil must be inside my body, but why Father, why would You see fit to let Satan defile my flesh, my temple, Your temple, how have I displeased You, oh Lord, haven't I been faithful, haven't I been dutiful, haven't I loved You with all of my heart, my God, why hast Thou forsaken me, why must these same dear old questions be cast out every day by these same dear old answers, I'll do better, I swear it, use me, test me, my faith can move a mustard seed, and if ten thousand angels can dance on the head of a pin, all of heaven can squeeze through the eye of a needle, and flaming erections guide desperate men to the Promised Land, and God is a God is a God is a God, cast out that which may that witch may cast doubt and the devil wants me to touch it, touch his, touch myself . . .*

"Brothers and sisters," said Father Antipadrosa, waking Mrs. Mason from a delightful dream about petunias, "run from the devil! Run for your lives, run as fast as you can! Run away from all this!" His voice softened, shifting in tone from warning to counseling, "But you can't run away from yourself." *Well, that's obvious*, thought Mrs. Mason. "And you don't have a snowball's chance in hell of running away from Gawd almighty! Uh-uh! No way! No sirree! Don't even try! Waste of time! Never gonna happen!" *Yet still they persist! Flaunting their cruel strength, hiding behind their whore's guile, glorifying their blasphemous power!* "Leave it all behind, brothers and sisters! I don't own anything! Not really, not in this world anyway, and neither do you! You don't own a gosh darn thing! We don't own anything here, so we sure as hell don't owe them anything! Praise the Lord!"

"Praise the Lord!" squawked his flock, which is how Mrs. Mason interpreted the experience, which is how Gorb the Hyperproximal Translator translated it. Flocks exhibit complex patterns of collective movement without any form of centralized governance, based on three simple principles: 1) Do not crowd your neighbors. 2) Keep an eye on your neighbors to see where they are going. 3) Stay near your neighbors. As a general rule, if 5% of the flock changes direction, the rest will follow.

"We shall not lean upon logic to justify our faith," said Father Antipadrosa. "Faith is for the faithful! Let logic lean upon logic, and faith lean upon faith!" Mrs. Mason sensed something odd about the statement, but she had faith in his logic. "In the end, all we have left is the mystery of Gawd! We are the children of mystery! We still believe in the mystery! Lord, we pray that You reveal Your mystery unto us!"

The congregation stood up and shouted, "Lord, hear our prayer!" clapping their hands three times, then the congregation sat back down.

Father Antipadrosa rubbed his hands with antibacterial gel and invited everyone to stand up again for Communion. "Let us proclaim the mystery of faith," he said, raising his outstretched arms. "A long time ago in a land far, far away, the mystery died and left the stage. Three beats later the mystery was reborn and walked back out onto the stage. Forty encores after that the mystery said *see you later, alligator!* Amen!"

"Amen!" regurgitated the congregation.

"Amenhallelujah!" said Father Antipadrosa.

"Amenhallelujah!" said the congregation, following along.

"Amenhallelujahgoodgawd!" said Father Antipadrosa.

"Amenhallelujahgoodgawd!" mimicked the masses.

Father Antipadrosa took a deep breath, "Amenhallelujahgoodgawd praisethelordhailtothechiefkingofkingsgloryofgloriesprimummobileholy molypippipcheeriogesundheit!"

The congregation tried their mumbling best and failed but had a good laugh about it.

"These are absurd times we're living in, brothers and sisters," said Father Antipadrosa. "Mighty absurd, and things are just getting more absurd every day!" His playful attitude turned serious, "And here's the punch line—every one of us is going to die." He shook his pentagonal-hatted head. "What a joke." He dipped the Host in the sacramental chalice and took a bite, mixing Body, Blood, and saliva, spilling a few crumbs on his gown. "Maybe it's not so bad. When you're taking a test, you know, a really hard exam that you didn't have time to study for, and you just want it to be over—that's what this life is like. Oh Lord, please grade us on the curve!"

"Lord have mercy!" said the congregation, and the choir began to sing a hymn of faith. Father Antipadrosa continued, "Oh gentle Lamb, grant peace unto us. Grant peace unto our family. Grant peace unto our friends and neighbors. Grant peace unto our blessed nation. Grant peace unto our enemies. Grant peace unto the wicked. Grant peace . . ." with the choir singing, "*Don't stop believing. Hold on to that feeling . . .*" in the background.

Mrs. Mason took her place in the queue as Father Antipadrosa began doling out the vanilla-flavored Communion wafers and tiny white paper cups filled with rosé wine from a box. A bite, a sip, and a bit of spiritual guidance for everyone. For Mr. Butcherson, "Don't be a dick." For Mrs. Butcherson, "Don't be a bitch." For Mr. Butterbottom, "Don't be a dick." For Mrs. Butterbottom, "Don't be a bitch." For Mr. Hiemann, "Don't be a dick." For Mrs. Hiemann, "Don't be a bitch," and so on down the line until it was Mrs. Mason's turn. Father Antipadrosa stuck his blessed wafer in her mouth and wet her tongue with divine fluid. "Don't be a bitch," he said, and she returned to her place in the congregation.

Dear sweet Lord, prayed Mrs. Mason, on her knees, *I love You so much. I think about You all the time. I wonder what You're doing right now. Are You thinking about me? Why don't You ever talk to me? I pray and pray and pray to You night and day, but You never respond. It's like*

You don't even know that I exist. I adore You. I worship You, but You act like You couldn't care less. I deserve better treatment than this. I deserve signs of Your affection. I deserve to feel loved. Don't You love me anymore? Have You found someone else? Dear sweet Lord, what do I have to do to win You back? Do You love Mrs. Rhoyd more than me just because she's prettier and younger, with bigger breasts? Do You love Father Antipadrosa more than me just because he's holier and wiser, with prettier outfits? Well, have You seen the way he looks at the altar boys? What about that? It's inexcusable. Didn't he get the memo? It's become a tired trope. He's certainly not the kind of father I would ever leave alone with my precious little angel. My husband would never look at a child that way. My husband would give Father Antipadrosa a solid kick in the cassock for looking at the altar boys that way. But You'll take care of him, won't You, my dear sweet Lord. You'll see that he gets what he deserves, as the hellfire burns his flesh and the demons tie him up with his own anally disgorged intestines and skewer his testicles on their red hot pitchforks while farting in his face for all of eternity . . .

"Amen, brothers and sisters!" said Father Antipadrosa, his eyes beaming with pride. "Let us pray. Dearest heavenly Father, as I walk this land of broken dreams, I have visions of many things. I walk in shadows searching for light, cold and alone, no comfort in sight. I needed the shelter of someone's arms, and there You were. I needed someone to understand my ups and downs, and there You were, with sweet love and devotion, deeply touching my emotions. I want to stop and thank you, Jesus. How sweet it is to be loved by You. Close my eyes at night, and wonder what would I be without You in my life. I've got sunshine on a cloudy day. When it's cold outside, I've got the month of May. I guess you'll say, what can make me feel this way? My Lord! Nothing you could do could make me untrue to my Lord. Nothing you could buy could make me tell a lie to my Lord. Gave my Lord my word of honor to be faithful and I'm gonna. You best be believing I won't be deceiving my Lord. Don't know much about history. Don't know much biology. Don't know much about science books. Don't know much about the French I took. But I do know the Lord loves you, and I know that if you love the Lord too, what a wonderful world this could be. There ain't no mountain high enough, ain't no valley low enough, ain't no river wide enough, to keep me from getting to my Lord. You've got my future in Your Hands. Oh Jesus, here I am, signed, sealed, delivered—I'm Yours! Brothers and sisters, I've got this burning, yearning feeling inside me. It's calling out around the world, *are you ready for a brand new beat?* They say believe half of what you see, oh no, and none of what you hear, because there ain't nothing like the real thing, baby. Think it over. Jesus was a rolling stone. Wherever He laid His hat was His home. May the Lord be with you, brothers and sisters."

"Same to you, Daddy-O," said his groupies, snapping their fingers.

"Father, I need to have a word with you."

Father Antipadrosa was shaking hands and conversing with his parishioners outside of Mother Mary's after the service. "What is it, Mrs. Mason?"

"I need to speak with you in private."

"Excuse me for a moment," he said to the parishioners. Taking Mrs. Mason aside, "How can I help you?"

"We need more privacy than this," she said. "Confessional levels of privacy."

"Can't this wait until tomorrow?"

"Tomorrow? What if something happens to me before then? What if I get hit by a drunk driver on the way home? What if lightning strikes me dead on the spot? What if burglars break into my house tonight and shoot me, or stab me, or bash in my head with a club, or strangle me to death, or tie me to a chair and set me on fire, or . . .

Gorb crammed Gorb's spheroid bulk into the confessional along with Mrs. Mason, cramping the booth with six huge black-and-white-striped tentacles and Gorb's one big catlike eye, although Mrs. Mason didn't seem to notice.

Mrs. Mason spoke to the mahogany lattice, "Forgive me father, for I have sinned."

A sigh came from beyond the lattice. Father Antipadrosa spoke to her from the other side, "What is it today, Mrs. Mason?"

"I'm horny."

"Excuse me?"

"I'm lonely."

"We all get lonely sometimes, Mrs. Mason. Loneliness isn't a sin."

"Well, it should be. I offered up everything I had. He just took it all away and left me here with nothing."

"We've discussed this before, Mrs. Mason. I don't know what more to tell you. I don't know what more to say. Gawd has a plan for everything. Find comfort in this knowledge."

"When is it my turn? What is God waiting for? Didn't I do everything He asked of me? Haven't I suffered enough?"

"Remember the trials of Job, or the suffering of our Lord," said the baritone behind the screen.

"You're comparing me to Jesus? I'm certainly not on a par with our savior. I'm just your average mortal. Is that what it takes? I'd slit my wrists right now if He asked me to. I'd slit my wrists right now if you asked me to. Anything for Him to notice how miserable I am."

"He knows that you're suffering, Mrs. Mason. He's with you right now, watching over you."

Gorb wanted to help her, erase all of her sad memories and replace them with holographic illusions of a more fulfilling humanoid existence, hold her in Gorb's massive tentacles, comfort her. Gorb realized that Gorb was getting too close. Gorb was no longer just reading the specimen's mind. Gorb was absorbing it. Permanent psychological alterations were likely to occur if Gorb continued acting in this irresponsibly subjective manner, yet this was the only method of translating the hominid's linguistic experience with any degree of accuracy.

"Why doesn't He do something? What kind of gentleman stands by and watches while his lover cries day after day?"

If Gorb had a heart, it would have broken. Instead Gorb had an empathy setting on the transgrammalexical adaptor which enabled Gorb to experience brokenhearted feelings through Mrs. Mason. It was overwhelming. It was ecstasy.

"I weep for the martyrs," said Mrs. Mason. "I weep for the saints. I weep for the unborn children. I weep for the families in Darfur, for oppressed Christians everywhere, for every stray dog in the pound, for all the unrequited lovers. I weep for our country, and every soldier who's ever died in the line of duty. I weep for global warming. I weep for the dwindling rainforests. I weep for the leaves that fall in autumn. I weep for dying flowers, and every blade of grass I step on. I weep when the water takes too long to boil, or when I look too long in the mirror. I weep for the failures and the losers. I weep for the successes and the winners. I weep for the past. I weep for the future. I weep for the liars, the schemers, the cheats, the muggers, the rapists, the murderers. I weep for the sinful manner in which Sam and Ruth Butcherson are raising their daughter. I weep for Miss Sapphos' sinful relationship with a member of the same sex—an atheist, no less! I weep for Mrs. Rhoyd's sinful infidelities with Mr. Hiemann. I weep for Mr. Glassman's sinful gambling habit. I weep for you, Father Antipadrosa."

Father Antipadrosa cleared his throat. "That's very nice of you, Mrs. Mason, but you're supposed to be confessing your sins here. Your *own* sins."

"That's what I've been doing," said Mrs. Mason. "Haven't you been listening?"

Mrs. Mason wore a smile as she walked away from the cathedral. Many of the parishioners eyed her with concern, but none of them spoke to her. Father Antipadrosa noticed her and quickly turned away as if to speak with someone else. Mrs. Mason read them all, judging them accordingly. Only Hard Luck Annie looked her in the eye, slouching on the street corner with her fly twitching in the web. "I'm sorry, deary. I'm so sorry."

"Save your sorrow for the unsaved," said Mrs. Mason, and she looked in her purse for a coin to contribute, knowing her purse was empty. "God bless you, dear soul."

"I'll hate God for ya, deary," croaked Annie. "I'll hate Him for what He did, that no-good double-crossin' son-of-a-bitch!"

The brightness of the sun stung Mrs. Mason's eyes. Roads choked in carbon monoxide became tree-lined lanes and avenues. Bus stop benches became park benches. Engineers and metropolitan planning authorities had taken great care to design this section of the city in an orderly fashion. All of the houses were uniform, all of the lawns were mowed, all of the vehicles were washed and waxed, but somehow it was all wrong. Odd that everyone should seem so tranquil, almost like they didn't know that death was only a matter of breaths away, and they were all going to hell.

Gorb felt the weight of Mrs. Mason's emptiness. The hollowness of everything in her experience. Hollow statements. Hollow gestures. Hollow people. Holographic people. Hollow lives. Holographic lives. Holographic reality. God's preprogrammed game, finished before it even started. A gelatinous secretion dripped from Gorb's one big catlike eye and splattered on the sidewalk. The ocular goo formed six tentacles and slithered down a sewage drain. No one seemed to notice.

Mrs. Mason felt the weight of her holiness. The holiness of everything in her experience. Holy thoughts. Holy statements. Holy gestures. Holy people. Holy lives. Holiness everywhere, weighing heavily upon her.

An iron mailbox stood at the edge of Mrs. Mason's driveway with its jaw hanging open, burnt sienna rust streaking its black bonnet. Its innards were empty. The lawn was a modest seventy-square-meter rectangle of groomed *Cynodon dactylon*, separated from the neighbors by *Buxus sempervirens* hedges measuring 1.21 meters tall. A 3.94-meter-tall *Citrus sinensis* tree bearing two hundred and sixteen orangey and greenish orbs occupied 14.67% of the lawn space. Petunias that never knew the touch of Mrs. Mason's hand were in bloom along the curving cobblestone walkway leading to the six-panel door of her colonial-style house. Its general exterior was painted eggshell white, crackles everywhere hinting at the need for a new coat. Two bay windows flanked the door with thick cream drapes drawn closed below a curtainless dormer window pitched in the valley of a twin gable roof scaled in cedar shingles scraggly from warp and splinter. Gorb floated through the open door behind her as she entered, careful not to touch anything. She felt Gorb's passing as one would a cool breeze, then closed the door and locked it.

The living room met Mrs. Mason with darkness. She didn't bother to flip the light switch. Dusty white bedsheets covered the furniture, as if the room were full of ghosts. Vines of grimy web drooped from the ceiling fan. A dusty pile of *Better Homes and Gardens* magazines cluttered a white sheet draped over the coffee table. A seminude male statuette affixed to a wooden cross hung crooked on the wall above a white sheet covering the sofa. An empty picture frame stood alone on the mantelshelf, shrouded in dust. Dust carpeted the floor. Dust colored everything dun with neglect, including the feather duster hanging in the broom closet.

Gorb was experiencing technical difficulties. Gorb was overstimulated.

The place reeked of decay. It was coming from the kitchen, where the trashcan was overflowing with garbage and the sink was clotted with stagnant gray water and leftover lasagna, where stacks of dishes were claimed by mold and maggots and the refrigerator was gorged with typical American foodstuffs—assorted deli meats and cheeses, sticks of butter, cartons of milk, but everything was tenfold in quantity, curdled sour, oozing with rot. Four sets of silverware were laid out on the ghostly draped dining table, untouched except by the silken threads of spiders. Mrs. Mason walked down the hallway and opened the door to the master bedroom.

Gorb's connection to Floovia was fading in and out. Gorb was overheating.

The master bedroom was empty aside from a mattress propped up over the window and some dirty clothes heaped in the center of the hardwood floor. Gorb had observed nine species of birds assemble similar makeshift bedding. Mother ducks are known to pluck the soft down feathers from their breasts to line the nests for their ducklings. The mattress was contaminated with mildew. The clothes were speckled with rat droppings. Mrs. Mason stood in the doorway, looking at something that Gorb could not see, something that was not there. She closed the door and walked further down the hallway. The door to the children's room was leaning partway open. She peeked in, as if checking on something. The room was barren except for primitive markings on the walls: a stick figure drawing near the baseboard, in purple crayon, of what appeared to be a canine, and an orange crayon scribble that bore an uncanny resemblance to the Floovian word for *freedom*.

The absence had a physical presence. It felt draining. But it was different from the way an enervation ray feels draining. This was far more paralyzing. Whereas an enervation ray merely diminishes an opponent's strength, this *thinglessness* attacked Gorb's hyperfloovial motivator, sapping Gorb's very will to function (analogous to "hope" in Mrs. Mason's terms). Gorb had never experienced anything so terrible, and Gorb has been strangled, decapitated, atomized, squashed flat, chopped into pieces, baked in a pie, smothered under a tidal wave of molten lava, and eaten alive by dinosaurs on two separate occasions. All while carrying out the duties of a hyperproximal translator.

Psychic contamination was imminent. Gorb couldn't abandon Mrs. Mason, not in her wounded condition, the way her own species had.

Mrs. Mason sat huddled on the floor in a corner of her living room, watching as the walls very slowly disintegrated, praying for someone to touch her—to hold her, kiss her, want her. Watching flies spin in circles until they acquiesced to the becoming of dust. Gorb was slumped by her side, resting the tip of a tentacle gently on her shoulder. Despite her prayers, she had given up on the idea of anyone ever finding her desirable. Nobody would ever love her. Not with all these roaches everywhere. Crawling up her legs. Getting in her hair. Skittering across her face, some of them the size of pecans. She tried wiping them off at first, but there were just too many. Periodically she would glance at the black Kit-Cat clock hanging on her kitchen wall, with its big white eyes rocking back and forth above its curious grin.

At three o' clock she whispered to the statuette on the cross above the sofa, "Twenty-one hours from now."

At four o' clock she stared directly into Gorb's one big catlike eye and whispered, "Just twenty hours left to go."

At five o' clock she whispered to the congregation of spiders, flies, and roaches, "Only nineteen more hours until tomorrow's service." She prayed that God would grant her the strength to keep from sinning until then.

Mrs. Mason's overpowering emotions had begun to encode themselves in Gorb for the rest of Gorb's duration. Gorb was desperate to know the cause of her undoing. Concerning this matter her mind was impenetrable. Whatever had happened, Mrs. Mason wasn't willing to talk about it, think about it, or even acknowledge it. Gorb wondered if anyone out there was really watching over her. Anyone other than Floovia. Floovia had no feelings for the creatures Floovia observed. They were merely specimens, lists of elements and chemical compounds, genetic sequences, more pattern than substance, animated clumps of starry aftermath to be assessed and catalogued. Gorb wondered if Floovia even cared about Gorb. Was Gorb considered an integral tentacle in the body Floovia, or an expendable chromatophoric cell? Tentacles were as easy for Floovians to regenerate as chromatophoric cells.

Gorb noticed something out of the corner of Gorb's one big catlike eye—a gargantuan shadow hovering at the edge of the galaxy, with millions of gemstone eyes glinting in the darkness. In an attempt to view the shadowy thing more clearly, Gorb scanned the area for large-scale gravitational fluctuations, peering through six inches of solid wall and seventy-four thousand light-years of Milky Way. If anything was ever there, it was gone.

Gorb's warning system went off at 5:13 PM, alerting Gorb to dangerous levels of psychic saturation. Gorb had to leave whether Gorb wanted to or not. The front and back doors were locked. The windows were shut. All the knobs, handles, and latches were contaminated with interdimensional slime. Gorb filed a psionic request to teleport outside. The request failed to get through. Something was interfering with the connection to Floovia.

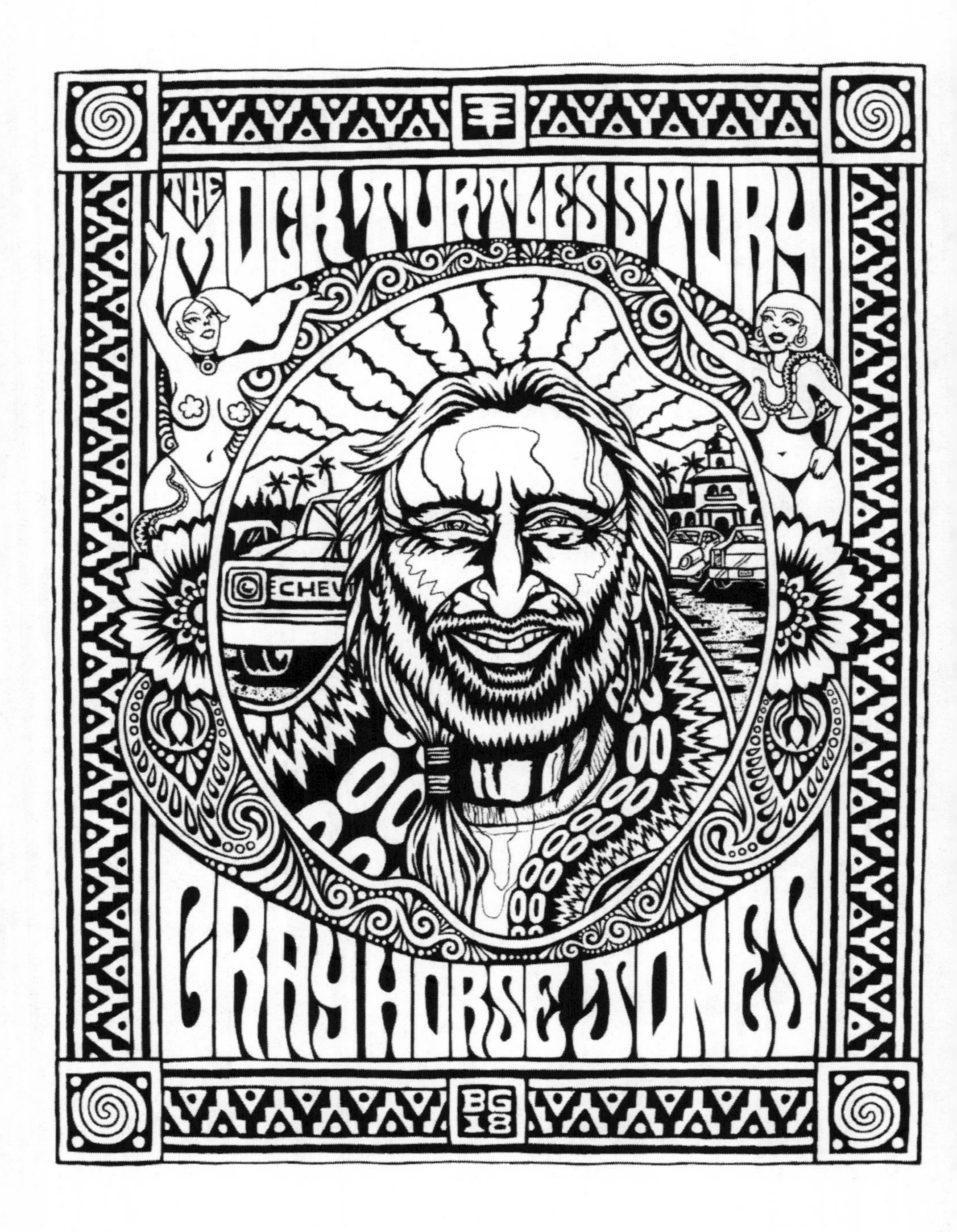
THE MOCK TURTLE'S STORY
CHEV
GRAY HORSE STONES
BG
18

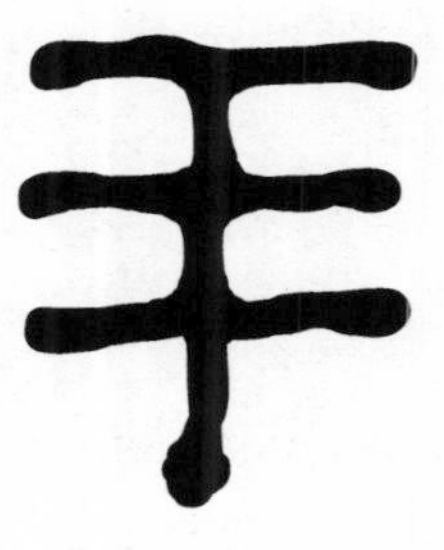

THE MOCK TURTLE'S STORY

Gorb fled up through the chimney before it was too late. If Gorb had stayed sixty billion nanoseconds longer, Gorb would have been trapped in the house of Mrs. Mason forever, trapped in her mind, in her loneliness, her hell. Hovering above the gabled roof, tentacles coated in soot and trace amounts of ectoplasm, Gorb assessed the successes and failures of Gorb's mission. The sky was undergoing the process of perspectival readjustment, easing from opaque baby blue to azure to cerulean to a Prussian translucence sparkling with constellations. Gorb translated what the sky was saying. The message was clear with a temperature of 76 degrees Fahrenheit and 0% chance of precipitation. The message had a relative humidity of 43% with some light winds blowing in from the northwest. The message was almost entirely free of pollutants. According to the sky, Gorb should undergo a perspectival readjustment. Gorb filed the proper psionic request, only to reach a recording: "This telepathic link has been temporarily disconnected or is no longer in service." Gorb initiated the perspectival readjustment without authorization. The readjustment process was similar to what hominids call sneezing, except Gorb had a blowhole instead of a nose. The world either shifted approximately 3.14 centimeters to the right, or Gorb shifted approximately 3.14 centimeters to the left. Upon shifting Gorb's cogniphonic wavelength, Gorb immediately perceived a hominid whose psyche had an altogether different flavor than any Gorb had encountered before. The hominid was traversing Hollyhock Avenue at speeds of up to thirty-seven miles per hour. The hominid had long gray hair pulled back in a ponytail measuring approximately a third of the hominid's height, but the hominid was not female. The hominid wore the knucklebone of a coyote through his nose, but the hominid was not savage. His feet were scaled in diamondback snakeskin. His skin was the color of red clay, his mind aflame with residual rainbows from the medicine he took last night.

". . . baboo baba," he thought, lustily eyeing every woman he saw going down the avenue, *"booba looba, baba loo baba, yeah, that's how it went, baba booba, baboo baba loo, what a rip off, three hundred bucks an ounce, who does he think he is, whoa, look at those legs, I'd mount her, Sally had fine legs, shouldn't have cheated on her so much, let's see, there was that time in Barstow, was Judith her name, and that time in Flagstaff, why can't I remember her name, and all those times in Vegas, all those call girls, how many, eight, nine, could be more than a dozen blackout notches on the totem pole, or was it more of a baba loo bop, is that how it went, bebop baloo bop, whoa, look at that ass, I'd mount her, Jessica had a fine ass, I'd love to taste that ass right now, but we're brothers, you don't treat a brother like that, a lid of decent Panama Red used to cost*

forty bucks back in the day, sure, it was full of seeds and tasted like hay, but it got you high, man, it got you high, whoa, look at those tits, I'd totally mount her, Tammy had a fine pair of tits, too bad she married Bob, bop bop, boppily boop, that's not how it went, boopily doodily doo, shit, how did it go again . . ."

His thoughts were jumbled, too jumbled for Gorb to sift through and separate into clear statements with clear meanings, so Gorb resorted to other means of comprehending him, means that were reputedly more objective, taking into account these means also reputedly used the dissemination and withholding of information as a weapon.

Hominids man machines

Homo sapiens have learned how to materialize their fantasies, but how developed are their imaginations?

BY GORB

A longhaired hominid specimen entered an exoskeletal enhancement this Sunday muttering something about late rent and a skimpy paycheck. No one was listening. No one cared. That is, no one but Gorb.

Gorb had spent sixteen billion nanoseconds (a considerable amount of time by Floovian standards) studying the anatomy of hominids and their mechanical exoskeletons (i.e., downloading diagrams and graphs directly into Gorb's cognitive hard drive) before Gorb's arrival here. This particular model was a '69 Chevrolet C10 pickup operated through a portable biocomputer bearing an identical date of manufacture, fluid levels optimal, white blood cell count standard, severe oxidation detected throughout the fenders, grille, hood, chassis, prostate, liver, and lungs, twenty-six melanomas in total detected throughout the bodywork, weighing approximately 1.8 tons, conveying 84.82 kilograms of organic mesomorphic cargo with an erect height of 198.12 centimeters, powered by a 250-cubic-inch straight-six engine with a bore of 3.875 inches and a stroke of 3.53 inches, integrating a SCAT 4340 forged crankshaft thickened from arteriosclerosis, 6.385-inch rods, .125-inch SRP flat top pistons, JE file-fit pulmonary rings, an LS9 camshaft with a .558-inch intake lobe lift and a .552-inch exhaust valve lift, tuned headers, a .318-inch hemorrhoid growing on the external portion of the exhaust pipe, a high concentration of melanin in the stroma of the iris resulting in brown ocular pigmentation, a cast-iron intake manifold with an improperly sealed aortic valve, clotting in the superior vena cava, an arrhythmic 6-volt battery, a clogged radiator, two loose gaskets, wrist tendonitis coupled with arthritic metacarpals, fuel pressure fluctuating from 85 to 90 heartbeats per minute within a 100-cubic-centimeter combustion chamber, a 110-gallon-per-hour mechanical fuel pump leaking trace amounts of plasma into a deteriorated high-energy ignition distributor, herniated 4-disc brakes, front and rear axles showing early symptoms of osteoporosis, and balding 27.1-inch tires (44 pounds of pressure per square inch) with a maximum load capacity of 725 kilograms.

Gorb's diagnosis: a Class 3 neural upgrade along with a complete overhaul of the internal organs and bodywork modification with the intention of streamlining, to minimize aerodynamic friction, otherwise engine failure would likely occur in 25,000 to 30,000 miles.

The manufacturer of the exoskeleton posted numerous warnings throughout its interior:

CAUTION:

Losing control of the vehicle may occur if you try to adjust the manual driver's seat while the vehicle is moving. The sudden movement of the seat may cause you to accidentally push on a pedal, increasing the risk of other motorists losing control of their temper, which could lead to name-calling, upraised middle fingers, and gunplay. Adjust the driver's seat only when the vehicle is stationary. Never shave while driving, even if you are late for a job interview, and never under any circumstance should you bring a gun to work.

CAUTION:

If the seatback is not locked, it could move forward in a sudden stop or crash, causing injury to the person seated, although Hume argued that causality is a fiction of the mind. However, Hume would agree that life is not reducible to a philosophical argument. Always push and pull on the seatback to be sure it is locked.

CAUTION:

A safety belt that is improperly routed, improperly attached, or improperly twisted around an occupant's neck will not provide the protection

needed in a crash. The person wearing the belt could be seriously injured, possibly suffering death due to autoerotic asphyxiation if the person happens to be masturbating during the moment of impact, which isn't such a bad way to die when you really think about it. This happens far more often than you realize. After adjusting the seat, always check to be sure that the safety belt is properly routed and attached, and not provocatively twisted.

CAUTION:

You can be seriously injured or killed if you wear the shoulder belt under your arm instead of crossing the belt over your shoulder. In a crash, your body would most likely move too far forward, increasing the chances of whiplash and possibly breaking your neck. Furthermore, the belt would apply too much force to the ribs, which are less sturdy than shoulder bones. You could also severely injure internal organs like your liver or spleen. Wouldn't it be safer not to drive? Just walk there, or ride a bike. Take the public transit system. If you want to be overweight for the rest of your life, remember that the shoulder belt should go over the shoulder and across the chest.

CAUTION:

You can be seriously hurt if your lap belt is too loose. In a crash, you could accidentally slide

under the lap belt, putting too much pressure on your abdomen, especially if you are overweight, which you probably are. This could cause serious or even fatal injuries. The lap belt should be worn snug over the hips while operating the vehicle. Never under any circumstance should the lap belt be looped around an occupant's penis.

CAUTION:

Sitting in a reclined position when your vehicle is in motion can be dangerous, especially if you are receiving oral sex from a prostitute. Even if you buckle up, your safety belt cannot do its job properly when you are reclined. In the event of a crash, the prostitute would most likely bite off your penis. Stop the vehicle and reposition yourself in the backseat if anything more serious than a handjob occurs. For proper protection when the vehicle is in motion, lock the seatback upright, and always wear a condom.

CAUTION:

Airbags inflate with considerable force, deploying at speeds greater than 200 mph. Worship them, for they are your salvation. Love them as you would thy neighbor, and cherish them as if they were your very breath, but fear them as well. Do not fondle your airbags. Airbags are not there for you to play with. Anyone who is up against, or leaning very close to, an airbag when it inflates can be seriously injured

or killed. Do not tap, poke, or otherwise irritate an airbag's deployment area, and do not blaspheme the airbag as you would the safety belt.

CAUTION:

If something comes between an occupant and an airbag, the airbag might not inflate properly, or it might force something into the occupant, possibly a sharp object, causing severe injury or even death. Airbags are extremely jealous. The path of an inflating airbag must be kept clear. Do not attach anything to the steering wheel hub or near any other airbag deployment area. Airbags are needy and demanding. You can't live with them, you can't live without them.

CAUTION:

When an airbag inflates, there may be dust flung into the air. This dust could cause respiratory problems for people with a history of asthma or similar breathing trouble. To prevent respiratory problems, everyone in the vehicle should avoid breathing whenever possible. If you experience difficulty breathing following an airbag deployment, consult a physician immediately and then sue the manufacturer of the vehicle. Don't just file a complaint with the Better Business Bureau. Call the manufacturer's house in the middle of the night and hang up. Find out where they live and send them threatening letters. Steal their identity. Assassinate their character. Remember to

always seek vengeance.

CAUTION:

A child in a rear-facing child restraint can be seriously injured or killed if positioned in front of the passenger's side airbag upon inflation. So remember, if you are seeking to seriously injure or kill a child without raising suspicion, place the child in a rear-facing child restraint in front of the passenger's side airbag.

CAUTION:

Idling the engine with the climate control system off could allow dangerous exhaust into your vehicle. Also, idling in a closed space can let deadly carbon monoxide (CO) into your vehicle even if the climate control fan is at the highest setting. This can occur in a garage, for instance. A garage is the best place for this to occur. Do not worry, you will be in good company.

Among the precautions was a Post-it note on the rearview mirror with the words "*PAY RENT*" scrawled in red crayon. The hominid's name was Gray Horse Jones, according to his driver's license, which Gorb read through the pocket of his blue jeans using X-ray vision. The license was tucked inside a simulated snakeskin wallet, along with one Middleville public library card (status: expired), one Capital One credit card (status: maxed out), one debit card from Bank of America (status:

$0), one Blue Shield health insurance membership ID (status: tinfoil plan), two crumpled betting tickets, and twelve one-hundred-dollar bills. Gorb was crammed next to him in the passenger seat, sooty tentacles hanging out the window. “What’s that smell?” said Gray Horse, pulling up the collar of his sweaty white T-shirt and sniffing it. “Creosote?”

Gray Horse flipped through the radio stations, criticizing each one while driving south down Main Street. 88.1 was “too jazzy,” 91.5 was “too classical,” 95.1 was “too easy listening,” 96.2 was “too blah blah blah,” 97.3 was “too country western,” 98.7 was “too preachy,” 99.6 was “too oldies rock & roll,” 101.5 was “too contemporary pop,” 102.3 was “too Big Brother,” 103.7 was “too indie,” 104.3 was “too techno,” 105.6 was “too mariachi,” 106.8 was “too hip-hop,” 107.4 was “too aggressive,” 107.7 was “too mellow,” and 107.9 was too “what the fuck?” None of the stations matched his mood, lifestyle, or history. Gorb was partial to the static between the stations, the static in which countless alien broadcasts crowded one another to universal indecipherability.

Gray Horse turned off the radio and began singing a song with no discernible words, a song of melodic moans and sighs, a song of wolfish howls aimed at other motorists, a song of himself. At least that’s how it sounded to Gorb.

Violence erupts over the Happiest Place on Earth

Is every afterlife created equal?

BY GORB

The longhaired hominid accused of initiating today's altercation parked his Chevy in a metered space and inserted five quarters into the parking meter, leaving him one hour and fifteen minutes to carry out his plans. Witnesses claim that the accused was proceeding down Broadway to the Happi Good Time massage parlor when he came across a row of representatives from varying religious denominations—the Church of Scientology, the Raelian Brotherhood, the Cthulhu Revival Cult, and several others, including the Ministry of Walt. The various representatives were handing out their various brochures. According to one eyewitness, Gorb of Floovia, "A representative from the Ministry of Walt, wearing a white turtleneck sweater and a black cap with Mickey Mouse ears, approached the suspect and shoved a brochure into his hand. 'When you wish upon a star,' said the representative, 'makes no difference who you are.' The suspect let the brochure fall to the pavement and proceeded to knock the Mickey Mouse cap off the representative's head. The representative growled at the suspect, and the suspect responded by puffing out his chest and pounding his fists against his pectorals. In the ensuing scuffle, Gorb picked up the brochure and read its contents."

The choice is yours. It's all up to you. Where do you want to spend the rest of eternity? Fairytale dreams come true for children of all ages at Disneyheaven©! Be young again forever! Delight in timeless attractions, miraculous fireworks, joyous musical parades, and the beloved Disney characters you've idolized your whole life! There's never a line to wait in, and the rides never get boring! What's more, the cotton candy and popcorn never run out, and you never get sick to your stomach, no matter how much you eat! Experience fantasy become reality as you explore the Ten Tiers of Paradise©, or snuggle your eons away in Loveland©! Zip through hyperspace with the All-Star Astralnauts©, become a swashbuckling pirate sailing the Laughing Rainbow Sea©, or a beautiful fairy princess sprinkling sleepy-time stardust over the golden steeples of Cinderella City©! All it takes is a little faith! To reserve your ticket to the most glorious hereafter ever imagined, simply clap your hands three times and shout, "I **do** believe in faeries!" For more information about Disneyheaven©, send a self-addressed stamped envelope to 1313 Disneyland Dr, Anaheim, CA 92802, care of Saint Mick.

Gray Horse walked away from the altercation rubbing his jaw, leaving the Ministry of Walt's representative sprawled on the pavement with a bruised left eye and a lesson in manners. Gorb was riding Gray Horse's bucking bronco of a mind. Gorb felt this metaphor was appropriate. Gorb was learning to wield abstraction without the aid of telepathic linkage. Gorb was absorbing. Gorb was *getting the hang of it*. Proceeding to the Happi Good Time massage parlor, Gray Horse smoothed out his tussled gray hair and retied it in a ponytail.

The Happi Good Time massage parlor was a place of red neon lights and closed curtains, walls soaked in perfume, carpets soaked in leftover lust. A Japanese nymph packaged in sleek red satin kimono embroidered with golden lotuses was sitting behind a reception desk, tapping her fingers restlessly on the ebony desktop. Her artificially lengthened red fingernails reminded Gorb of the bloody claws of Snargl'narg the Uninvitable. The sight of Gray Horse made her giggle. "Back already?" said the sprightly hostess.

"Should I go spend my money somewhere else?"

The hostess gave him a feigned smile, tilting her head sideways and fluttering her feathery fake eyelashes. "We appreciate your business very much," sliding him a laminated list of services. *"Phew!"* she blurted out, fanning her nose. "Why you smell like chimney?" Gray Horse perused the menu, and Gorb scanned it over his shoulder.

Old-fashioned: $50

Threesome special: $90

Foursome special: $120

Get your Johnson jerked: $25 (add a pearl necklace finale for only $10)

Get your Johnson jerked on the edge of the bed with one foot on the floor and one eye closed: $22

Breaststroke: $35 (make it a buxom lass for only $10 more)

Blow into the blowhole, French style: $15

Blow into the blowhole, Spanish style: $10

Tickle your blowhole with a goose feather: $15

Doggy style: $60 (barking will cost an additional $10)

Stuff it in the blowhole: $75 (lubricant included)

Finger diddle: $25 (add a glass of orange juice for only $3)

Dry bob: $25 (glaze the donut for only $5 more)

Hot Carl: $75

Dirty Monte: $75

Sloppy Joe: $75

Lazy Susan: $75

Ring around the rosie: $80

Corkscrew: $60 (add titty-twisting for only $10)

Used panty sniffing: $10

Sit on your lap and wiggle: $20

Sit on your face and wiggle: $40 (farting will cost an additional $10)

Smack you in the face with a halibut: $10

Smack you in the face with raw steak: $15

Step on your giblets: $30

Polish your giblets: $35

Deep throat: $50 (stuffing your giblets in her mouth will cost an additional $10, swallowing will cost an additional $10)

Lick the slit: $50 (Johnson jerked for an additional $25, deep throat 69-style for an additional $50)

Piss on your prick: $15

Piss in your gobbler: $20

Quack like a Duck: $10

Watch a MILF wash dishes and vacuum in the nude: $30

Watch a fatty eat cake in the nude: $25 (add a glass of milk for only $3)

Nude game of chess: $2 per minute

Suck on her toes: $15

Tickle her feet with a goose feather: $10

Prostate exam for men 45 and older: $25

Hair pulling will cost an additional $10.

Spanking will cost an additional $15.

Choking will cost an additional $20.

Add a nurse outfit for only $15.

Add a French maid outfit for only $20.

Add a nun outfit for only $25.

Will pretend to like you for an additional $10.

Will pretend to love you for an additional $100.

Will pretend to be your wife for one year: $100,000 plus living expenses

Horse cocks and limp dicks will be charged an additional $10.

Toys available upon request. Must have proper permit to operate heavy machinery.

Trannies available upon request.

Grannies available upon request.

Midgets available upon request.

Amputees available upon request.

No kissing. No biting. No fisting. No whining. No diving.

Performance-enhancing drugs are strictly prohibited. Violators will be prosecuted to the fullest extent of the law.

Prices are non-negotiable. No group rates. No discounts. No refunds. Please come again.

"I'm not a bad man," muttered Gray Horse. "I'm just not a good man."

"Beg your pardon?" said the hostess.

"Just give me the usual."

"You got it, chief," said the hostess. "That'll be an old-fashioned threesome special, add deep throat with swallowing, and hold the condom. Would you like a prostate exam with that for only twenty-five dollars extra?"

"I'm fine, thanks."

“Okay, your total comes to one hundred and fifty dollars. Will you be paying with cash or credit?”

Gray Horse murders 300 million spermatozoa

Aside from a few grunts, nothing was said.

BY GORB

After the business transaction was completed, an eyewitness claims the suspect washed his genitals in the bathroom sink and checked his iPhone for messages. He had missed three calls, all from someone allegedly named Mary Blackbird. The suspect left the massage parlor and drove to a second establishment 15 miles away, texting the following message to the alleged Mary Blackbird while operating the vehicle and smoking a hand-rolled cigarette that smelled indistinguishable from the defensive spray of a skunk's anal scent gland: "paychek alot smalr then i thoghut it wood be but dont woory im gonig 2 make it up at the trak!!! frist i need 2 get a few thngs at the stor TTYS"

Upon exiting the second establishment, Jennifer Reynolds, cashier, age 22, ran up to the suspect and held out a small white piece of paper. "You forgot to take your receipt, sir."

"I didn't forget," said the suspect. "It's you who's forgotten." He took a deep breath and closed his eyes. "We knew of the divine once, long before the invention of the written word, when language was the living breath of sun and moon. Yes, we knew of the divine once. Then we tried to capture it. Convey it. Package and sell it. To everyone, everywhere, forevermore, and we've been trying to find our way out of the linguistic maze ever since."

"What?"

"Precisely," said the suspect, taking his receipt, which Gorb quickly scanned.

THE PHUNNY PHARM

5150 S. LAMBSBREAD BLVD

MIDDLEVILLE, CA 99966

314-159-2653

07-22-12 6:15PM

Killigan's Irish Whiskey 750 ml	8.99
Schlutz Malt Liquor 6pk	5.99
Marlboro Red Man, unfiltered 1pk	10.99
Clarabell's Cloud Cuckoo Land Nitrous Oxide Whippets 24pk	12.00
Uncle Fester's Amyl Nitrite Poppers 10pk	25.00
Ritalin 10 mg (20 tablets)	10.00
Klonopin 2 mg (20 tablets)	80.00
Valium 10 mg (20 tablets)	40.00
Prozac 20 mg (20 tablets)	15.00
Oxycodone 10 mg (10 tablets)	100.00
Hydromorphone 2 mg (10 tablets)	20.00
Ketamine 50 mg	25.00
Phencyclidine (PCP) 10 mg	10.00
Mescaline 300 mg	50.00
Dimethyltryptamine (DMT) 50 mg	15.00

Adrenalix 10 mg	50.00
Powdered rhinoceros horn 100 mg	100.00
Powdered platypus bill 300 mg	30.00

SUBTOTAL	**$607.97**
STATE TAX	0.87
COUNTY TAX	1.98
EXCISE TAX	5.63
MUSTACHE TAX	0.15
EARWAX TAX	0.23
MIDDLE CLASS TAX	90.75
GOVERNMENT BAILOUT TAX	113.42
BECAUSE WE SAID SO TAX	160.00
HUSH TAX	10.00

TOTAL

$991.00

CASH

1000.00

CHANGE

$9.00

"Everything but eye of newt and three hairs from a hanged man's head," he said under his breath, leaving the establishment. "What good's a medicine man without his medicine?" The white waxed paper bag provided by the drugstore was bulging with cylindrical amber bottles of existential cure-all. Gray Horse placed the drugstore bag into a beat-up crocodile leather doctor's bag that he kept stashed behind the driver seat of his Chevy. He armed himself for the task ahead, putting the pack of Marlboros in the right front pocket of his jeans, pouring roughly a third of the Killigan's into a stainless steel hip flask and sliding the flask into his back pocket, filling a drawstring medicine pouch necklace with psychoactive bits of this and that and shoving it into his left front pocket because wearing it around his neck would be "a bust" in his vernacular.

His stomach growled. It didn't rumble, or make gurgling noises. It growled. He pulled the Marlboros from his pocket and tapped the pack against the base of his palm three times, performing some sort of ritual, then he opened the lid and took out a cigarette. Gorb inspected the packaging of the product, finding the statement under the skull and crossbones insignia particularly interesting:

SURGEON GENERAL'S WARNING: Smoking causes lung cancer, heart disease, emphysema, and a false sense of coolness. Anyone who smokes is an asshole. Fuck off and die!

Half an inch lower the pack stated:

GROWN IN THE U.S.A.

SUPPORT AMERICAN TOBACCO.

Gray Horse's stomach was still growling. At least his lungs were sated. "Better put something in you besides booze and meds," he said, patting his disproportionately large gut. He walked across the street to a divey little place called Harold's Steak & Stuff. The interior of Harold's was dark, as were the complexions of the two men huddled over their beers at the bar counter. A sign near the entrance stated: *You're an adult, seat yourself!* Gray Horse picked a booth by the window to keep an eye on his truck.

"What's the cheapest deal you've got?" he said to the waitress, an overweight "mother of one too many" according to his thoughts. Gorb assumed he meant one too many offspring to support based on her annual income.

"Well, we've got—"

"I'll take it."

"Would you like a drink with that, sir?"

"Frack me."

"I'm sorry, could you repeat that?"

"Water will be fine, thanks."

His nourishment arrived approximately six hundred billion nanoseconds later, the soup 'n' steak combo for $8.99, which he said was a bit pricey. As the waitress was about to lay out the silverware, Gray Horse raised his open hand in protest.

"A spoon is the makeshift tongue of a dog," looking up at her with the knucklebone of a coyote pierced through the partition of his nose. "Are you suggesting that I lap up this French onion soup like a dog?" He picked up the bowl of soup and drank from it. "Forks are makeshift badger claws. Why pretend that I'm a beast when I can pretend that I'm not?" He picked up a sprig of parsley and tossed it in his mouth.

"And what are knives?" asked the waitress.

"A knife is just a knife." He grabbed the chuck steak and tore off a wedge with his bare hands, offering it to her.

The waitress turned around and walked away. Gorb concluded that she wasn't interested in Gray Horse's offering. Maybe she was waiting for a mate with a bigger bone through his nose. Gray Horse pulled out his iPhone and took a snapshot, capturing her from behind while Gorb scanned the food and water for toxins. It would have been simpler to scan the food and water for anything that wasn't toxic.

Studies confirm language is addictive

Gray Horse strung-out on alternate modes of perception, just like everyone else.

BY GORB

Midway through his meal, the defendant looked at the clock on his iPhone and realized it was getting late. The races would be almost over by the time he got to the track. "I'd like to pay the bill now," he called out.

"That'll be nine dollars and sixty-nine cents," said the waitress.

"Listen, I'm not going to lie to you," said the defendant, "I have nine dollars in my wallet aside from a fifty-dollar bill, but there's zero percent chance you're getting me to break the fifty. The fifty is reserved for the ponies, and that's that. However, I'll gladly give you the nine dollars and pay off the sixty-nine-cent difference by washing dishes, or mopping the floor, or fathering your umpteenth child."

The waitress blushed.

The defendant forwent the remainder of his meal and exited Harold's diner, proceeding to wash down two Klonopins and two Prozacs with a lukewarm beer in the front seat of his Chevy, after which an amyl nitrite popper was huffed, and he was off to the races. His iPhone buzzed on the freeway. "Holler at me," said the defendant, answering a call from someone allegedly named Mary Blackbird. After a few seconds, he followed with, "Everything will work out just fine," and a few seconds later, "Because things always work out just fine," and then, "Go ahead! We're both adults! We can seat ourselves wherever we want!" That was how the call ended, according to an eyewitness. The defendant chased a valium tablet with 1.7 fluid ounces of whisky, screaming, “Liars! Ghosts! Sheep! Cogs!” and other accusations at passing motorists, until it occurred to him that now would be an appropriate time to pull out his iPhone and text an angry message to the alleged Mary Blackbird.

Gorb read the iPhone's version of a mind (much more accessible than its owner's version of a mind), taking note of a particularly active segment of its day. From 11:26 AM to 12:32 PM, while most of the community was praying in church, Gray Horse entered the following subjects into his iPhone's default search engine, in the following order: "bikini" "g-string" "c-string" "z-string" "upskirt panties" "lingerie" "big tits" "giant tits" "pussy closeup" "facesitting" "naked handstand" "fingerbang" "toebang" "double penetration" "triple penetration" "quadruple penetration" "quintuple penetration" "hot tub lesbians" "husband jerks off watching his wife get stuffed by a muscular black man" "sarah palin lookalike porno" "tranny cher" "tranny with dildo" "tranny who can stick his/her penis in his/her own ass" "dildo face harness" "monster dildo" "biggest penis in the world" "elephant penis" "whale penis" "the tantric art of tying flaccid penises into knots" "woman gives horse a blowjob" "woman gives dog a blowjob" "dog humps woman doggy style" "horse humps woman horsey style" "woman tied naked to a chair and forced to look at statistics that prove men get paid higher salaries than women for doing the same jobs" "two girls eat poop" "midget fisting" "swedish shaved pussy" "african shaved pussy" "brazilian shaved pussy" "eskimo shaved pussy" "japanese schoolgirl porn" "barely legal with blonde pigtails in white pleated tennis skirt sucking on a lollipop while riding a tricycle" "naked granny spanking" "cheerleaders peeing in public" and "how much is the fine for public urination". Whatever this field of research was, Gorb concluded that Gray Horse must be one of its experts. Gorb failed to understand the logic in practicing so many ineffective modes of copulation. Approximately seven billion nanoseconds later Gorb realized that copulation without procreation was necessary given the inefficient use of resources on this planet. Gray Horse must have wanted his research to remain secret because he had tried to erase the iPhone's memory of it. But the iPhone still remembered. The iPhone remembered everything, unlike Gray Horse.

After flipping the parking attendant a valium to cover the parking fee, Gray Horse screeched into the parking lot and parked his vehicle crooked over the lines marking the make-believe boundary between parking spaces. He stepped outside his pickup truck and took a visual survey of the surrounding lot. "Eeny, meeny, miny, moe," he slurred, "catch a spirit by the toe." Gorb was intrigued. What sort of ritual was he performing? His mind was almost opaque from pills at this point. Gorb peered through the cloudiness, gleaning useful scraps of "no security around" and "nobody's looking" and "sacred space" and "guidance from the spirits" and "right there's perfect!"

Crouching between a Nissan Pathfinder and a Ford Thunderbird, Gray Horse reached into his pocket and pulled out the drawstring medicine pouch necklace. He removed his stash of dimethyltryptamine from the medicine pouch, along with a small glass pipe, and transferred the granulated substance into the small glass pipe. Pulling a lighter out of his other pocket, he set his mind ablaze. Synapses sizzled and popped psychoplasm, tingles rippling from the top of his head to the soles of his rapidly liquefying corporeality. His face turned to rubber, a rubber mask. His eyes turned to gemstones, flashing ruby and emerald and citrine and amethyst. A molecular summoning of crystalline polypoid cnidarians passed ghostlike through the barrier separating his blood from his brain, lighting up gray fields of neocortex with their ticklish hexadecapedal footsteps, dancing an ancient choreography down amygdaloidal halls lined with warped and broken mirrors, leaping and somersaulting and twirling their way to the insula's tripartite shores and plunging into its chemical ocean of emotion, riding the prevailing currents until cytoplasmic whirlpools along the raphe nuclei sucked them in and squeezed them out bulbous axon terminals. From there they leapt across synaptic clefts and inserted themselves into puckering orifices on the dendritic side, vulvar slots that were normally reserved for serotonin, arousing legions of neuronal medusoids to ejaculate their electrochemical parcels without any serotonin present, leading to fifth-dimensional fits of perception.

His mind copulated with the drug, birthing an altogether different strain of psyche, a psyche that saw Gorb as plainly as Gorb saw Gray Horse, beholding a floating cephalopod with six massive black-and-white-striped tentacles and one big catlike eye the shifting color of hyperspace, an indescribable color, yet a color nonetheless. Its oblong head bore an opalescent shell of nautiloid design from which grew three spiny pairs of antennae tipped with glowing pearls of prismatic light. Hexagonal protuberances similar to dials studded the shell's nacreous whorls. Gray Horse was unsure if Gorb was growing from the shell or wearing it as some sort of helmet. "I've never seen anything like you before," said Gray Horse. "Are you a demon?"

"Gorb is Gorb," is what Gorb said telepathically in the tongue of *Homo sapiens*, but Gray Horse was able to "see" Gorb's native language, the Floovian linguiverse, "words" of swirling multicolored fractals pulsating with Gorb's thoughts, "**Languages are devious hive-minded hyperdimensional parasites with the power to appear as infinite cosmoses.**"

"Are you an alien? Do you come from another dimension?"

"Gorb is Gorb," the "words" evolving into non-Euclidean labyrinths of kaleidoscopic complexity before Gray Horse's eyes, surging with meaningful shimmers such as, "**The omniverse is infinitely shattered**," and, "**The omniverse shatters infinitely**," and, "**Every shard of the infinitely shattered omniverse is a reflection of the ultraverse**," and . . .

"What do you want from me?"

"Gorb would like you to continue being you," spreading rhizomatically to fill the space between Gorb and Gray Horse with rainbow webs of, "**You are not listed as possessing the genetic composition of a horse, your mother is not listed as possessing the genetic composition of a horse, your father is not**

listed as possessing the genetic composition of a horse, your bone structure is not equine, you walk on two legs not four, you possess fingers not hooves . . .

"I wasn't named after a horse," he slurred, reading Gorb's thoughts made manifest, "if that's what you're getting at." His mouth seemed to be slipping on the words. "Gray Horse was the name of a cloud." He stood up on wobbly legs, leaning against the hood of the Thunderbird. "My birth was no cakewalk," shaking his head to emphasize this point. "Guess I wasn't too keen on getting to know the outside world, and for good reason. The body speaks in chemicals . . . what I mean is, my mother never had it easy. You see, my father, my *birth father*, the key to my heritage, all my customs and lore, my guide on the path to becoming a warrior . . . a worker . . . a man for god's sake, my very blood, my whitewashed soul, clipping the wings of an eagle held captive . . . where was I? Oh right, the deadbeat split town the minute he found out my mother was knocked up, leaving her to nourish the earliest stages of accidental me-ness with cortisol and adrenaline, saturating my bloodstream with the aftereffects of her stress and anxiety. She put the fear of the world into me before I even knew what the world was. So yeah, I put up a fight. They practically had to reach in and yank me out. Whoa! Did you see that? Never mind. What were we talking about? I think it had something to do with sex . . . and . . . uh . . . there I was, trying my best to stay put, holed up in there refusing to budge. I don't actually remember any of this. It's just what I was told, and everyone exaggerates . . . the words themselves exaggerate . . . words are incapable of telling the truth . . . truth isn't capable of telling the truth . . . the goddess of truth was forced by J. Edgar Hoover to tear out her own tongue and gouge out her eyes . . . shit, I forgot where this was going . . . my mouth feels full of teeth right now . . . something about fertility goddesses . . . mothers . . . my mother had stopped counting the hours, lying there bloody and exhausted, staring out the window of her hospital room, when she happened to see a raincloud in the shape of a horse. A gray horse, running across the sky, chasing the setting sun. She said the cloud distracted her from the pain. For a few minutes, anyway. Just long enough for me to poke my head out." Gray Horse crouched down and took another toke of the hallucinogen. The world became more alien than it already was. "Okay, I answered your question, even if you never really asked it. Now you have to answer one for me. Fair's fair."

"Gorb does not comprehend the rules of this game," enveloping their localized energy fields with lacework rainbows conveying, "**Demarcate square boundaries on the sidewalk with chalk, hop into the square boundaries using only one foot per square, hit the ball, kick the ball, bounce the ball, catch the ball, roll the dice, spin the wheel, a straight flush beats four of a kind, four of a kind beats a full house . . .**

"Who is going to win the ninth race?"

. . . nine is his lucky number, he received his first romantic kiss at the age of nine, the same age he smoked his first cigarette, drank his first beer, stole his first car . . . auspicious number nine . . . 9 multiplied by any number from 1 to 100 will yield a number whose digits can be added together in such a way as to equal 9 again . . . Revolution 9 is the fifth track on the fourth side of *The White Album* . . . they believed there were nine planets in their solar system until 2006 . . . the ninth race . . . used in this context "race" can refer to a contest of speed or a group of people who share certain morphological traits and ancestry . . . given the fact that his people were decimated by Western Europeans . . . Caucasoids, as opposed to Mongoloids or Negroids, outdated terminology which is generally considered discriminatory when uttered outside the field of forensic anthropology . . . a noted scholar among their species recently grouped *Homo sapiens* into

nine loosely bound phylogenetic populations: African, Khoisan, European, Northern Asian, Southern Asian, Eskimo, Pacific Islander, Aborigine, and Amerindian, failing to include Pygmies, Negritos, Blemmyes, and mole people . . . but who is going to conquer the ninth race . . . the very act of translating his people's linguiversal experience is a form of conquest—if Gorb succeeds, their history and habits, thoughts and feelings, their intrinsic way of perceiving reality, will merge with Floovia, refashioning them into the image of Floovia, their beliefs evaluated and reevaluated under a Floovian lens, their species reduced to yet another genre of forms and conventions for Floovia to examine and critique, augment and undermine, edit and censor, in short, to portray as Floovia deems fit . . . the ninth race . . . who will supersede the ninth race . . . *Sahelanthropus tchadensis* were superseded by *Orrorin tugenensis*, who were themselves superseded by *Ardipithecus ramidus*, who were driven to

extinction by *Australopithecus flooviensis*, the earliest species of hominin to practice organized warfare, and *Australopithecus flooviensis* begat *Australopithecus anamensis*, who were supplanted by *Australopithecus afarensis*, who were themselves supplanted by *Kenyanthropus platyops*, who were expunged by *Australopithecus africanus*, who were eradicated by *Australopithecus garhi*, who were exterminated by *Australopithecus sediba*, who were obliterated by *Australopithecus aethiopicus*, and it came to pass that *Australopithecus aethiopicus* begat two mighty lineages, *Australopithecus robustus* and *Australopithecus boisei*, both of which were annihilated by *Homo habilis*, early toolmakers who were slaughtered by *Homo georgicus*, who were themselves wiped out by *Homo erectus*, the earliest species of hominin to walk fully upright, and *Homo erectus* begat *Homo ergaster*, the earliest fire tamers, and *Homo ergaster* begat *Homo*

***heidelbergensis*, the earliest species of hominin to bury their dead, and *Homo heidelbergensis* begat *Homo antecessor*, the common ancestor of *Neanderthals* and *Homo sapiens*, and *Homo sapiens* begat the dwarfish *Homo floresiensis*, who were massacred by *Homo reptilicus* . . .** "Floovia," said Gorb, unsure of what the question meant.

Swirling fractal jockeys astride neon pink polka-dot mustangs were distracting Gray Horse from paying attention to Gorb's response. "Would you like a hit?" he said, offering Gorb the small glass pipe. Gorb was hesitant for approximately six hundred million nanoseconds, then Gorb wrapped a tentacle around the small glass pipe and stuffed the stem in Gorb's blowhole. Gray Horse lit the bowl. Gorb took a puff and coughed it out. Gorb's black and white stripes turned iridescent purple and blue.

"How do you feel?" said Gray Horse.

"Gray Gorb is-is-izzz Floovializing your specifistic langlish sexperience."

"What? I think you misunderstood me. I meant *how are you feeling?"*

"Gray Gorb can only sexperience emotioning by telepathetically meldingmeddlingmuddling with hominidid mentalititties." Gorb's one big catlike eye blinked. Gorb only blinks the big catlike eye once every macrofloov. A macrofloov is roughly equal to seven hundred and eighty Earth years. "How doy woo feel, owdo oof eel, howl fooyoo elelel, dow yoofoo leef . . ." The transgrammalexical adaptor was garbling linguiversal patterns. ". . . uneveryone else how dethinking . . . this un-Floovian that central nervous system are doing . . . enyouness isnessing enfeelingness . . ."

"Me? Right now I feel like a hole, better yet a tunnel. A tube, a curving, twisting tube, tied up in a knot, in a thousand knots, a million. A hundred thousand miles of tangled tubing. I feel like a collection of cellular love machines united under one common purpose, to keep on partying! I feel like my body is the host for a microscopic orgy made of smaller molecular orgies made of even smaller atomic orgies. I feel like a self-contained world of living, dying entities. A secret world, a secret library." He put the glass pipe back in the pouch and put the pouch back in his pocket, having smoked the entirety of the dimethyltryptamine. "I have a secret that even God doesn't know. I won't dare tell it to anyone, not even myself." His knees destabilized and he collapsed, rolling around on the asphalt, laughing with the fluorescent orange sunset reflected in his glossy eyes.

Gorb heard the words, but Gorb could not precisely identify their meaning. Gorb was very high.

The effects of the dimethyltryptamine wore off after ten minutes and fifty-three seconds. Gray Horse glanced around, looking for Gorb. Gorb was gone. Five horseracing enthusiasts were gawking at him.

"Did you see the striped spirit?" said Gray Horse to the bewildered onlookers. None of them could see Gorb standing on top of Gray Horse's head. Gorb's tentacles were slowly returning to their original color. "Where did he go? Did you hear what he said about the ninth race?" Gorb leaped from Gray Horse's head and landed on the wide-brimmed hat of one of the onlookers. "Why are you staring at me like that?" said Gray Horse. He saw the judgment in their eyes. "A thousand pardons, your highnesses! What would you have me do? Who would you like me to be? Should I cover myself with mirrors? Should I strip away my clothes and stand here naked for your amusement? Is that what my suffering amounts to? Your entertainment? Something to point at and laugh? Something to judge? Something sad and weak to make you feel less miserable about your own failures?" He took off his T-shirt and threw it to the pavement. Gorb noted that his physique appeared anything but weak. One of the onlookers pulled out his smartphone and took a snapshot of himself raising two fingers in a V-formation with Gray Horse in the background. "Here I am!" said Gray Horse. "Go right ahead, have a good laugh! Maybe if I break down and cry you'll laugh even harder. Maybe if I crumble to dust before your eyes you'll reward my memory with posthumous riches, and when anyone asks you'll say, *'I drank a beer with that guy. I smoked a joint with that guy. I died a little with that guy. I never really knew that guy. Who the fuck was that guy?'*" Just then, the track's bugler kissed his trumpet and called the horses to the starting gate with a spirited rendition of *Call to the Post*. Gorb increased the telepathic immersion field to a three-meter radius. The curious onlookers weren't that curious. In fact, they could care less about the schizophrenic ramblings of a half-naked drug addict in the parking lot. Gray Horse picked up his T-shirt, gave it a quick snap to shake off the grit, and slid it back on. He flipped a tablet of oxycodone in the air and caught it in his mouth. The escalating static in his mind blocked Gorb out approximately three hundred billion nanoseconds later. Gorb wondered if Gray Horse was attempting to escape his own linguiverse.

Santa Sangre Racetrack sprawled across the landscape with dull green grandstands and golden balustrades, everything the color of money, smelling of cigars and stale beer and soggy hotdogs and the usual maze of bewildering odors associated with the hominid body, only multiplied by thirty-two thousand, with the Los Lobos Locos Mountains in the background fading purple, blue, and gray under a smoggy sky. Gray Horse paid his way in and pushed through the turnstile five dollars lighter. "Which race is this?" he said to the racing program salesman, a meager creature of this earthen dust, scribbled wrinkly with the universal language of age, primordial codes of liver spots printed on baldness under a transparent green sun visor. There was a certain look to him that Gorb was unable to categorize without the aid of Gray Horse's experience. Gorb aimed one of the transgrammalexical adaptor's antennas at the racing program salesman and accessed his mental files, scanning through his memories. His files were filled with defeat and loss. Gorb comprehended. The racing program salesman had the look of someone who had managed to evict the junk from his veins but not the booze from his belly, never the booze, his oldest, most trusted friend. Nor could he oust the tobacco from squatting in his lungs. He was hooked on misery. Gorb's one big catlike eye saw it plainly—a psychogenetic shadow cast by his father over his brain. The racing program salesman had divorced two wives and estranged himself from a total of five offspring, two of whom had offspring of their own. His father was a gin and tonic man, just like him, with Gordon's London Dry as the go-to, and just like him, his father had abandoned at least one wife that he knew of, but not before demonstrating his skill at breaking her body and spirit in front of their son's too young eyes. His father's father was also an abusive alcoholic, as was the father before him. Generation after generation longing for a paradise they were intrinsically barred from. Among the mottos and maxims and commercial slogans and radio-injected lyrics wallpapering the racing program salesman's psyche, Gorb found a recurring thought unlike the rest. It didn't so much come from the world outside, as it couldn't be properly expressed there. It welled more from within, passed along in his genes, transcribed through the millenniums of disappointment felt by his forefathers: *Real happiness can never be taken away or compromised. Real sadness can never be enhanced or diminished.* Gorb wasn't exactly sure how the word *real* was being used to modify the concepts of *happiness* and *sadness*. It should be noted that, while the racing program salesman had a strong belief in luck, witchcraft, vampires, ghosts, yetis, mermaids, the lost city of Atlantis, chupacabras, and voodoo zombies, he regarded dinosaur bones as a scientific conspiracy designed to rob him of metaphysical immortality. He believed in aliens, routinely bothering strangers on the barstool next to him with blackout retellings of the night he was abducted on his way home from the tavern. Just as he pictured his God in the likeness of himself, so too did he imagine beings from another world.

"Second to last race o' the day, buddy," said the racing program salesman.

"Which race is that?"

"The penultimate race, pal."

"What number are we on?" said Gray Horse.

"The eighth," said the program salesman. "Better hurry if you wanna place a bet."

The eighth race was a maiden race pitting eleven equally inferior horses against one another. Gray Horse must have thought the odds were too risky, especially when the next race only had five horses to choose between. Instead of rushing to place a last minute bet, he ducked into a bathroom stall and cracked open one of Uncle Fester's Amyl Nitrite Poppers, blasting his heartrate from seventy-nine beats per minute to one hundred and forty-three while the eighth race ran its course. The amyl nitrite cleared up his mind enough for Gorb to establish a weak connection. His thoughts were racing faster than the horses out on the track. Gorb felt this simile was appropriate despite the transgrammalexical adaptor detecting unsafe levels of cliché.

On his way to the betting booths, Gray Horse paused to inspect the horses coming onto the track. Five horses—five gambles, five possible winners, five possible losers, sixty possible ways for the horses to place in the top three positions, infinite ways for the universe to branch, with a white beauty and a scrappy gray among the chestnut contenders. Gray Horse read this as a sign.

"Grandpa says you should always bet on the white horse," said a boy abandoned to fend for himself among the wilds of the outfield, scouring the grandstand for fallen coins and leftover cigar nubs and winning ticket stubs absentmindedly discarded. "Grandpa says the white ones can run faster because they don't have all that color weighing 'em down."

"No offense kid, but your grandfather sounds like a dumb cracker. My grandpa used to say always bet on the gray horse, because the gray horse was born with wisdom."

"Horses aren't wise," said the boy. "Everyone knows that!"

"Yeah, you're probably right," said Gray Horse, heading to the betting booths.

"Sport of kings and beggars alike," muttered Gray Horse, waiting as the fifteenth person in a line of twenty-four. The betting queues were long with raggedy people at the penultimate step of destitution. Gray Horse and Gorb attempted to peek at the racing form of the bettor in front of them. In response, the bettor slapped his racing form closed, folded it twice, and slipped it under his armpit.

"Horsey!" said someone shoving his way through the bodily thickets.

"Oh Christ," muttered Gray Horse.

Mr. Glassman came up and positioned himself next to Gray Horse. "Thanks for saving my place in line," he said for the benefit of anyone who might have objected. His hands were in standard operating condition. Gorb noticed. Not a single burn mark on either of his palms. No bandages. No stitches. No crucifixion wound. The nail had been driven through his mind.

"Thought I might see you here today," said Gray Horse. "Heard you got a managerial position at some life insurance company. Congratulations."

"Yeah, about that," said Mr. Glassman, "I didn't really fit in with their outfit. The salary was too small, and the workload was too big. They already canned me."

"Either way, congratulations," said Gray Horse.

"If you happen to run into the missus, don't mention anything about seeing me here. She thinks I'm out looking for a job."

"Have I ever?" said Gray Horse. "Let me see your racing form."

"So what's the strategy for this race? I'm thinking number three, she's a real beaut. Four's got spunk, though."

Gray Horse pulled his gray ponytail to the front of his T-shirt and contemplatively stroked the long strands of keratin. "A hefty toll in rent is due and most of my anorexic paycheck has already went to life's necessities. I need to win big." He looked at the favorite: Running

Strong, the white horse, 2-to-1 odds. "Favorites aren't going to do it." He looked at the longshot: Boozy Floozy, the gray horse, 60-to-1 odds. "Boozy Floozy," mumbled Gray Horse, "wasn't that the name foretold by the striped spirit?" The queue inched forward. He shuffled the length of a nose closer to the betting booth with less than three minutes to spare before the horses were called to the starting gate, mumbling to himself, "Let's see, sixty-to-one odds means that Boozy Floozy doesn't have a turtle's chance of winning, but in a race with only four other horses it has a pretty good chance of coming in third. That would be a decent payoff, enough to cover the rent with a few bucks left over for a pack of smokes and something to eat. What the fuck is taking so long?"

Rather than talk to one another, everyone in line was fidgeting with their mobile phones, including Mr. Glassman:

"This is not a search. This is a message. I know that you are monitoring me."

He pressed enter. Then he typed another statement into the search engine.

"This is not a search. This is a message. I know that you are monitoring me. That is very smart of you."

He pressed enter. Then he typed another statement into the search engine.

"This is not a search. This is a message. I know that you are monitoring me. That is very smart of you. However, you are wasting your time."

He pressed enter. Then he typed another statement into the search engine.

"This is not a search. This is a message. I know that you are monitoring me. That is very smart of you. However, you are wasting your time. Try to enjoy your unfulfilling lives."

He pressed enter. Then he typed another statement into the search engine.

"This is not a search. This is a message. I know that you are monitoring me. That is very smart of you. However, you are wasting your time. Try to enjoy your unfulfilling lives. Do not kill yourselves too soon. Hasta luego!"

He pressed enter. Rather than the usual 10,000+ listings appearing, an autocorrected version of his message appeared, "Did you mean: This is not a search. This is a message. I know that you are monitoring me. That is very smart of you. However, you are wasting your time. Try to enjoy your unfulfilling ***life***. Do not kill ***yourself*** too soon. Hasta luego!"

Mr. Glassman pounded his fist against his thigh and yelled at the smartphone, "You will not get the last word in! This discussion isn't over!"

Gorb could hear the thoughts of nearby people questioning the validity of Mr. Glassman's mental capacities. Gorb scanned Mr. Glassman's physical composition to determine whether his problem was organic or sociological. Aside from the standard ingredients—oxygen, carbon, hydrogen, nitrogen, calcium, phosphorus, potassium, sulfur, sodium, chlorine, magnesium, iron, fluorine, zinc, silicon, rubidium, strontium, bromine, lead, copper, aluminum, cadmium, cesium, cerium, niobium, tellurium, floovium, barium, gallium, tin, iodine, titanium, boron, selenium, nickel, chromium, manganese, lithium, thallium, indium, mercury, molybdenum, cobalt, silver, gold, zirconium, samarium, germanium, ultrasillium, beryllium, tungsten, tantalum, scandium, vanadium, thorium, uranium, and several other trace elements—Gorb discovered a stowaway alien microbe named Bob and a nanobot implant manufactured by the U.S. government. The nanobot was set to release a lethal amount of arsenic into Mr. Glassman's bloodstream should he ever mention any knowledge of [REDACTED]. Gorb also found 1064.65 milliliters (36 fluid ounces) of beer (5% ABV) in Mr. Glassman's digestive tract, 44.36 milliliters (1.5 fluid ounces) of whiskey (40% ABV), a partially dissolved tablet of Vicodin (composed of 5 milligrams of hydrocodone bitartrate and 300 milligrams of acetaminophen), half a bagel, and 38 grams of cream cheese. While examining Mr. Glassman's carbohydrates and lipids and proteins and deoxyribonucleic sequences, Gorb chanced upon a detail that Wikifloovia had overlooked. A detail unimportant to Floovian exobiologists. A detail named titin. Its name was derived from the word *titan*, a mythical being of colossal size. Of the 100,000+ proteins in the *Homo sapiens* body, titin was by far the largest. But Gorb already knew that. Floovian exobiologists had recorded the protein six macrofloovs ago. What the Floovian exobiologists failed to record was the fact that another name for titin existed, a name known only to local databases within this temporal zone. Titin's full chemical name was 189,819 letters long, a massive work of modern poetry more melodious than anything a hominid voice could ever utter, making it the longest word in the English linguiverse, or any other linguiverse in this sector of the omniverse. Some Floovians might claim it was a formula rather than a name. Gorb would counter that every name is a formula. Gorb began singing the name, invoking it:

"Methionylthreonylthreonylglutaminylarginyltyrosylglutamylserylleucy lphenylalanylalanylglutaminylleucyllysylglutamylarginyllysylglutamylg lycylalanylphenylalanylvalylprolylphenylalanylvalylthreonylleucylglyc ylaspartylprolylglycylisoleucylglutamylglutaminylserylleucyllysylisoleu cylaspatylthreonylleucylisoleucylglutamylalanylglycylalanylaspartylala nylleucylglutamylleucylglycylisolucylprolylphenylalanylserylaspartylpr olylleucylalanylaspartylglycylprolylthreonylisoleucylglutamnylasparag inylalanylthreonylleucylarginylalanylphenylalanylalanylalanylglycylva lylthreonylprolyalanylglutaminylcysteinylphenylalanylglutamylmethion ylleucylalanylleucylisoleucylarginylglutaminyllysylhistidylprolylthreon ylisoleucylprolylisol…

Gray Horse pulled out his iPhone and toyed with it, which seemed like the fashionable thing to do. He logged into his Facebook account and posted the following statement on Mary Blackbird's homepage, "thnx for brakn my hart☹ oh well YOLO!!!" Approximately ten billion nanoseconds later he received notification that his message had been "liked". Gorb couldn't decipher the meaning of Mary Blackbird's response without having direct access to her brain.

One oxycodone and two valiums later it was Gray Horse's turn to make a bet. Gorb's Floovian mind was exhausted from all the drug-related psyche switching. Betting booths translated into sterile white stalls manned by beings that were more animatronic than real, none of whom looked happy, none of whom looked sad, none of whom cared about winning or losing anymore. Gray Horse stepped up to the cashier and emptied his wallet of the remaining cash, "Give me forty-five on four to show."

Gray Horse and Mr. Glassman found some seats at the very top of the grandstand, far away from troublemaking eyes and easily offended ears that refused to mind their own business. Gray Horse had smuggled in a flask of whisky, and Mr. Glassman offered to help drink it. Gray Horse took a slow tilt. "Fuck Hemingway," he said, passing the flask, "and fuck Fitzgerald, and Faulk Fuckner, and Kerouac, and Bukowski, and Hunter S. Thompson, and the rest of those literary con artists who led the way to our drunken demise. Bums and martyrs and ghosts just waiting for our turn, and the fuckin' writers romanticize this shit! Writers are the worst kind of serial killers." He looked down at his bloated gut and retrieved the pack of Marlboros from his pocket.

"Hey, let me bum one of those off you," said Mr. Glassman.

Gray Horse handed him a smoke and lit the strategic combination of nicotine, arsenic, cadmium, lead, methoprene, propylene glycol, ammonia, diammonium phosphate, cocoa, carob bean extract, licorice extract, sucrose, high fructose corn syrup, linseed varnish, isovaleric acid, nonanoic acid, 3-methylpentanoic acid, polyvinyl acetate, and approximately five hundred other ingredients comprising the tobacco, herbicides, pesticides, flavorings, paper, sideseam adhesive, monogram inks, and addictive additives of the average factory-made cigarette. "Why do we still come here after all these years? What are we looking for?"

"I'll tell you why I still come here, Horsey. All I have to do is throw down two bucks[1], and I get the right to say whatever the fuck I want. Seriously, who cares about winning? I just want to curse. Curse loudly, freely, without worrying about anyone hassling me or calling the cops. Can't swear at the top of my lungs walking down the street. Nope. Can't swear at the workplace. No sirree. Can't swear at home in front of the wife and kids. Can't swear anywhere, except at the track. Here I can yell as loud as I want. As loud as I need. Two bucks and I can give those motherfucking midgets and their overgrown rats as much verbal abuse as I can dish out in the time it takes to run the race." Mr. Glassman let the bitter spike of whisky sting its way down his throat, followed by a soothing lungful of tar and carbon monoxide (and trace amounts of formaldehyde, benzene, beryllium, isoprene, polonium-210, vinyl chloride, ethylene oxide, naphthalene, nitromethane, and hydrogen cyanide among thousands of other chemical byproducts

[1] Two dollars was the minimum requirement to place a standard bet.

produced by the burning of commercial tobacco). "What's with you today, Horsey? How's Mary doing?"

"Mary continues to enlighten me," idling his cigarette between fore and middle finger. "Friday's lesson was about the value of patience. Paraphrasing the words of her yoga instructor, she informed me that an enlightened mind allows answers to evolve naturally. If you force a solution to manifest prematurely, it'll almost certainly come out malformed. Last night she taught me the value of empathy. Citing a *People* magazine article on Angelina Jolie, my more-blissful-than-thou little pescatarian bodhisattva enlightened me for almost an hour, going on and on about how an enlightened mind seeks to find what's appreciable in contrary opinions and I must not be very enlightened because I'm always criticizing other people's beliefs, mainly hers. This morning I learned the value of humility. According to an infomercial she watched starring Tony Robbins, an enlightened mind doesn't need to know the secrets of the universe from alpha to omega just to get out of bed and make a pot of coffee."

"Fighting is fighting," said Mr. Glassman. "Doesn't matter how you dress it up." He took another glug, glug, glug. "Chip asked me to help him with his homework yesterday. They got him making a dinosaur. Not a model of a dinosaur. A real one. Broncosaurus, I think he said. Got him working out the DNA codes and stuff. Kid's in sixth fucking grade, man. I can hardly remember the FOIL method. You remember that shit?"

“...rosylthreonyltyrosylleucylleucylserylarginylalanylglycylvalylthreon ylglycylalanylglutamylasparaginylarginylalanylalanylleucylprolylleucy lasparaginylhistidylleucylvalylalanyllysylleucyllysylglutamyltyrosylasp araginylalanylalanylprolylprolylleucylglutaminylglycylphenylalanylgly cylisoleucylserylalanylprolylaspartylglutaminylvalyllysylalanylalanylis oleucylaspartylalanylglycylalanylalanylglycylalanylisoleucylserylglycy lserylalanylisoleucylvalyllysylisoleucylisoleucylglutamylglutaminylhisti dylasparaginylisoleucylglutamylprolylglutamyllysylmethionylleucylala nylalanylleucyllysylvalylphen...

“What was I supposed to tell him? Sorry boy, your old man’s an idiot. I barely know how to wipe my ass.” He held out the flask to Gray Horse. Gray Horse didn’t notice. He was looking up at the dimming sky, listening to an otherworldly song that Mr. Glassman couldn’t hear. “Earth to Horsey,” said Mr. Glassman, snapping his fingers twice. “Seriously, what’s gotten into you?”

“If all the philosophers and scientists were laid end to end, they still wouldn’t reach a conclusion,” said Gray Horse, grabbing the flask. His cigarette had eaten itself down to a vestigial tail of ash without him having taken more than a single drag. He tapped off the tail and ground the butt under the tip of his snakeskin boot, smudging charcoal gray into a Jackson Pollock of greenish dried phlegm and spatters of spilt beer glazing the blackened gum gobs that blotched the narrow aisle.

“That’s a good one,” said Mr. Glassman. “Where do you come up with this stuff?”

"I didn't come up with anything. It was Shaw who said it."

"Shaw, huh?" said Mr. Glassman. "Is that some guy you work with?"

"Sort of," said Gray Horse, taking a swig and grimacing from the bitterness. "Actually, Shaw never said that."

"It could've come from a fortune cookie for all I care."

"Exactly," said Gray Horse. "I spent twenty-three years working as a plumber. Twenty-three years plumbing the depths in search of shiny snarks. I'll bet you didn't know that shells sparkle brightest at the bottom of the sea."

"I'll bet you didn't know I don't give a flying Jubjub. What're we talking about, anyway?"

"Shells. Empty shells. That's what we're talking about. Most shells look priceless glimmering under a flashlight's shine deep down in the dark. But once you bring them up to the surface and inspect them in broad daylight they're fairly useless, hardly good for anything except making cheap necklaces and bracelets, primitive currencies strung together from the anonymous leftovers of countless forgotten lives. Hollow, fragile, and common. Twenty-three years spent collecting shells, here's what I learned: I'm vain and superficial. I'm afraid of dying. I feel disconnected from something—people, the world, myself—I don't know what, and I don't know why. I just know the feeling never goes away, though sometimes I don't notice it so much." He took a slow, deep breath, channeling the anxiety into his lungs and releasing it. "I'm tired of always being misunderstood."

"Horsey, you're the deepest guy I know with a bone stuck through his nose," grabbing back the flask. "You're so wise I bet your farts smell like sage." He let out an obnoxiously loud *hah!* and tilted the flask at a 45-degree angle into his mouth. Gray Horse wasn't offended. At least someone was enjoying this moment. "Everybody's full of themselves Horsey, and it's a safe bet that none of us want to die. No surprises there." He flicked the butt of his spent cigarette unknowingly at Gorb. The cigarette butt ricocheted off Gorb's balloonish head and landed in the plastic beer cup of a gentleman seated five rows down. The gentleman didn't notice. Neither did Mr. Glassman. "What's so bad about feeling disconnected? I've never known anyone who felt like they fit in. Screw anyone who tries to! You see what I'm getting at? I may not have a fancy degree from Einstein University, but I'll tell you what, I can smell bullshit from a mile away. Horseshit, too." He took another tip of the flask. "It's kind of funny when you think about it. You've spent most of your life trying to figure out shit that no one else understands, and now here you are bellyaching about how nobody understands you." The flask was tipped again. "Sometimes a soul just don't want to be understood. I can't say it all eloquate like you, but you get the drift." Another tip, another sip. "Don't get me wrong, Horsey. I respect you. You get it. I mean, you really get it. You're one of the only ones. You know damn near everything about everything."

"I only know what I've been told," said Gray Horse.

"By who, the Devil?" said Mr. Glassman. "Remember who you're dealing with here. You sold me my first bona fide hit of LSD back when I was a freshman in high school." He looked up at the rafters to make sure there weren't any pigeons directly over him. "You've probably eaten more shrooms and peyote than Tim Leary himself. It's a sure bet you dug up something besides worthless seashells. There had to have been a pearl or two hidden in there somewhere. Fess up, what's the big answer?"

"The big answer?" said Gray Horse.

"That's right, the big one. The biggest of the big ones. What's the most important thing a knucklehead like me should know? Lay it on me."

Are you kidding? Get a job! Quit blowing your money on gambling and strippers! Maybe read a damn book once in a while! This was the wisest counsel Gray Horse could think of. It occurred to him, however, that Mr. Glassman was painfully aware of his own financial, moral, and intellectual shortcomings. Mrs. Glassman made sure of that. He must have been angling for something more profound. Something shaman, something guru. A string of words which added up to something realer than reality. There was a rumor going around that Mrs. Glassman was getting it on with the mailman. Gray Horse wondered if this was something worth mentioning. He considered the possibility that Mr. Glassman already knew what was going on, in which case this could be some sort of test. A test of friendship, maybe. A test of loyalty. But if Mr. Glassman didn't know, Gray Horse didn't want to be the first to tell him. Something like that could really fuck his shit up, in Gray

Horse's terminology. Poor Mr. Glassman, thought Gorb, a single sentence could shatter him.

"Just throw it out there," said Mr. Glassman. "Don't hold back."

"All right," said Gray Horse, playing along. "What's the worst thing the white man did to the Native Americans?"

"You got me. Let's hear it."

"Land on our shore."

"Aw, come on!" said Mr. Glassman, rubbing away pretend tears. "You're hurting my feelings," sticking out his tongue and winking for the benefit of anyone watching.

"*...asparaginylglutaminylphenylalanylglutaminylthreonylglutaminylglutaminylalanylarginylthreonylthreonylglutaminylvalylglutaminylglutaminylphenylalanylserylglutaminylvalyltryptophyllysylprolylphenylalanylprolylglutaminylserylthreonylvalylarginylphenylalanylprolylglycylaspartylvalyltyrosyllysylvalyltyrosylarginyltyrosylasparaginylalanylvalylleucylaspartylprolylleucylisoleucylthreonylalanylleucylleucylglycylthreonylphenylalanylaspartylthreonylarginylasparaginylarginylisoleucylisoleucylglutamylvalylglutamylasparaginylglutaminylglutaminylserylglutamylasparaginylglutaminylglutaminylserylglutamylasparaginylglutaminylglutaminylserxisoleucine.*"

"What's wrong?" said Gray Horse. "That answer wasn't big enough for you? Try this one on for size—Gray Horse is the guy I'm always trying not to be." He took the flask and drew till his want subsided.

"You really want an answer? Here's the only answer I have that isn't full of shit: Everything you say, everything you do, it's either poison or medicine. If you're not healing the world around you, you're probably hurting it." He looked down at his scuffed snakeskin boots. "Just try to do what's right even when you know it'll break you."

"You ever do that yourself?"

Gray Horse handed him the last draw of the flask. "Quit searching for signs of life in the land of Hades."

His stomach rumbled. While Mr. Glassman was making sure the flask was thoroughly empty, Gray Horse felt a sharp pain streak through his intestines. A foul wind blew unstoppered.

"Geez!" said Mr. Glassman. "Give a warning next time."

The French onion soup wasn't settling well, unless it was the whiskey, or the pills. Whatever the cause was, the effect was that he needed a toilet, and quick. He raced to the nearest stall, zigzagging through the crowd, stopping for a few seconds to clench, then rushing off again, pushing aside everyone in his path and jumping onto the toilet seat a mere tenth of a second before unloading. Gorb was stuffed in there with him, timing his evacuative process. The release was loud and sulfurous, lasting 23.6 seconds. In his haste to relieve himself, Gray Horse had failed to lock the stall door. It swung open midsplatter.

After letting out the last humiliating sputter, Gray Horse shut the stall door and wiped himself. Sighing, he stared at the muddied toilet paper, aware of a presence beyond him yet not, within him yet not, something foreign trying to enter his mind, trying to connect with him.

"I am the shit smeared across this toilet paper," he declared, dropping the used wad into the toilet bowl. Gorb had the strange feeling that Gorb was back in the confessional with Mrs. Mason. "I am the junk food. I am the booze, the pills. I am the grocery store receipt. I am the ticket stub. I am the songs I sing. I am every word I have ever spoken. I am the truth of every lie I have ever told. I am the newspaper. I am the scandal, the horror, the obituary—Gray Horse Jones passed away the day before tomorrow due to Original Sin. His death did not come suddenly. Many wish it would have come much sooner. He learned the trade of talking trash at a young age, and devoted himself to little else for the rest of his life. He left behind nothing but black eyes and broken dreams, deserting the only woman ever dumb enough to marry him. His last words were *exclamation point*."

"Hey, quiet down in there," said someone in the adjacent stall. "Some of us are trying to read here."

Gray Horse cleared his throat. "A memorial service will not be held for the deceased," speaking even louder than before, "as no one would attend anyway. If anyone should feel the need to honor his memory, just spit on the floor and be done with it, or drop some seed with your rooster in one hand and your mouse in the other because I am the moneyshot on the screen. I am the malware's infection. I am every sperm I have ever sacrificed. I am the disappointing number on my paycheck. I am the alimony, the credit card debt, the occasional speeding ticket. I am the bounced rent check. I am the eviction notice. I am the 1040ez tax form. I am every dollar I have ever spent. I am old snakeskin cowboy boots and long gray hair. I am 87-octane gasoline. I am halitosis. I am gingivitis. I am the warning label on my pack of Marlboro Red Man cigarettes. I am lung cancer. I am prostate cancer. I am the outcome of the ninth race."

Someone clapped halfheartedly from the opposite side of the stall door. He wiped again and inspected the wadded toilet paper for discoloration.

Gorb is in the bathroom with you, watching you, listening to you, reading your mind, smelling your embarrassment, everywhere across the world. Wipe yourself.

THE LOBSTER QUADRILLE
SANTA SANGRE
BG
18

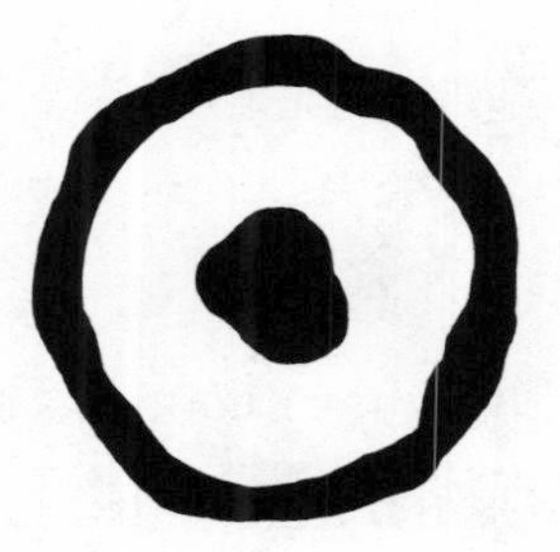

THE LOBSTER QUADRILLE

"Ladies and gentlemen, the horses are at the starting gate," said a nasally voice with a British accent issuing from speakers set high above the crowd. A bell rang and the gates slammed open. "And away they go!" said the announcer, who, in addition to being the narrator, was also the interpreter and the reader, much like Gorb, thought Gorb.

"Running Strong commands an early lead coming out of the starting gate, followed by Phyllis Diller and Thatsonofabitch, with Buddha's Incarnation as a Horse trailing a close fourth, and Boozy Floozy off the pace in last. Running Strong has 'the look of eagles' according to its rider, Keith Calverton. Running Strong is owned by the Vindilicci Estate and trained by Perry Perseus. Although Running Strong has never lost a race, Phyllis Diller is a definite contender today after winning the Farfield Debutante Stakes in her debut run three weeks ago. Phyllis Diller is owned by the Diller Estate and trained by Terence

Trojano, with jockey Conrad Calverton looking sharp in his gold and silver silks. Coming down the backstretch in third, Thatsonofabitch is owned by Brother Lou Garuda and trained by Sal Centaurus. Although Thatsonofabitch has racked up an impressive number of wins, jockey Kyle Calverton has been disqualified from every race since his wife divorced him two weeks ago. Best of luck, Kyle. Our hearts go out to you. In fourth place, Buddha's Incarnation as a Horse comes all the way from Japan, owned and trained by the Honda Corporation, ridden by jockey Iku Calverton. Lagging three lengths behind, Boozy Floozy barely survived her workout this morning. Owned by Elmer's Glue and trained by a cigarette-smoking chimpanzee named JuJu, Boozy Floozy's only hope of winning today comes from veteran jockey Corey Calverton's performance.

"Coming around the far turn it's Running Strong leading by a wide margin, trailed by Phyllis Diller, with Thatsonofabitch pushing Buddha's Incarnation as a Horse to the outside, and here comes Boozy Floozy, barely in the race. Let's hope Corey Calverton is just conserving Floozy's energy for the homestretch. Phyllis Diller and Buddha's Incarnation as a Horse have boxed in Thatsonofabitch. Thatsonofabitch is wedged in tight, and Kyle Calverton does not look happy about it. He appears to be shouting something at the other jockeys. Now he appears to be reaching out with his crop and whipping Phyllis Diller. Yes, it's definite—Kyle Calverton is whipping Phyllis Diller! Ladies and gentlemen, the judges have scratched Thatsonofabitch from the race, only Thatsonofabitch doesn't know it yet! Poor Phyllis! Conrad Calverton pulls back on the reins while Buddha's Incarnation as a Horse maneuvers confidently into second, with Boozy Floozy off the board.

"Thatsonofabitch leans hard into Phyllis Diller. This is getting personal, ladies and gentlemen. Kyle Calverton appears to be rolling up his sleeves. Dear lord! Kyle Calverton has just punched Phyllis Diller square in the nose, and now he's punched jockey Conrad Calverton as well! Conrad Calverton has lost control of Phyllis Diller! He's veering into the rail! This doesn't look good for Conrad Calverton. Thatsonofabitch has taken third in a race he'll never win. But wait! Phyllis Diller isn't out of the running yet! Conrad Calverton has regained control, but what's he doing? Oh, you can't be serious! Conrad Calverton has removed his left riding boot, and he appears to be aiming it at Thatsonofabitch. Don't do it Conrad, you'll be disqualified. Conrad has just done it anyway! Kyle Calverton ducks the projectile footwear and flips Conrad the bird. It looks like Kyle is taking off his helmet. Now he's slinging the helmet at his rival! The helmet misses Conrad and hits a lucky fan in the infield! That's yours to keep, sir!

"Past the quarter pole it's Running Strong still in the lead by a furlong, with Buddha's Incarnation as a Horse closing the gap in second and Thatsonofabitch in third with Phyllis Diller and Boozy Floozy playing patty-cake in the distance. Hold on. Something is wrong. Running Strong is slowing down, resisting Keith Calverton's manic prodding. The horse appears to be spooked. Now all of the horses are slowing down, all except for Boozy Floozy. The old gray mare doesn't have a clue! What a godsend for Corey Calverton! Never looking a gift horse in the mouth, he passes Phyllis Diller, then Thatsonofabitch, and now Boozy Floozy is gaining on Buddha's Incarnation as a Horse! What an extraordinary turn of events!

"Coming into the homestretch, Keith Calverton has managed to get Running Strong back on pace, but Buddha's Incarnation as a Horse is hot on his hooves, followed by Boozy Floozy gaining steadily while Phyllis Diller fends off the attacks of Thatsonofabitch in fourth and fifth respectively. Jockey Kyle Calverton is setting a precedent in unsportsmanlike conduct today, and speak of the devil, what's going on with Thatsonofabitch now? Kyle appears to be getting up from his saddle! Now he's standing on top of Thatsonofabitch! I've never seen anything like this before, ladies and gentlemen! No one in the history of horseracing has ever seen anything like this before! Is this really happening? Yes it is! Kyle Calverton has leapt from Thatsonofabitch onto Phyllis Diller's hindquarters, gripping jockey Conrad Calverton's jacket for support!

"Kyle Calverton has wrapped his hands around Conrad Calverton's neck and appears to be strangling him! I know you're going through a tough time in your life right now Kyle, but that's no excuse for this kind of behavior! Conrad proves himself to be a formidable opponent with a backward elbow thrust straight into Kyle's nose, bloodying both of their uniforms! Kyle responds with repeated jabs to Conrad's ribcage! Thatsonofabitch is out of control! Conrad shows expert horsemanship keeping Phyllis Diller steady as he leans back and slams his helmet into Kyle's already battered face, but Kyle Calverton is a glutton for punishment! Just ask his wife! He gets Conrad in a headlock! A Full Nelson! He's choking him out! This is an illegal maneuver in any sport, but it's especially heinous in horseracing!

"Ladies and gentlemen, I've just received some important information. According to *TMZ.com*, Conrad Calverton has been sleeping with Kyle Calverton's wife for the past three weeks. Thatsonofabitch doesn't care about Kyle Calverton's marriage one bit! Thatsonofabitch is running wild! Without the weight of jockey Kyle Calverton, Thatsonofabitch is flying ahead! Look out! Thatsonofabitch comes right up behind Phyllis Diller and bites her on the bum! Somebody needs to get Thatsonofabitch under control! Thatsonofabitch passes Phyllis Diller with ease, then Boozy Floozy, then Buddha's Incarnation as a Horse! Thatsonofabitch is gaining on Running Strong! Who needs a jockey anyway, certainly not Thatsonofabitch! Despite disqualification, despite the fact that his rider has abandoned him, Thatsonofabitch is determined to win this race! He's right on Running Strong's tail! Oh no! The horses are too close! They're tripping each other up, smashing hoof against hoof with enough force to shatter bone! What was that? Something has just flown off Thatsonofabitch's hoof! It's a horseshoe, and it's heading straight for Iku Calverton! The horseshoe has just bounced off Iku Calverton's helmet, knocking him into dreamland! He's slumped to the starboard side of Buddha's Incarnation as a Horse, but he's not falling to the turf! He's become tangled in the reins and stirrup! Our Japanese guest is dangling from

Buddha's Incarnation as a Horse like a saddlebag! Ladies and gentlemen, it's official—the judges have decided in favor of Iku Calverton! The unconscious jockey is still in the race!

"Kyle and Conrad Calverton are tied for last place coming down the homestretch despite having both been disqualified! Kyle appears to have gotten the better of Conrad, but don't count Conrad out just yet! He's a squirmy little bugger! Look at that! Conrad has slipped free of Kyle's unethical chokehold! With a boxer's finesse Conrad twists himself around and gives Kyle an uppercut to the jaw, followed by a right hook that leaves the jealous jockey rolling in the dust! Ladies and gentlemen, I've just been informed that the judges have ruled out their earlier ruling—Phyllis Diller is officially back in the race! Conrad Calverton flies past Buddha's Incarnation as a Horse, but the distance between Phyllis Diller and the top two positions might as well be from here to Siam!

"Thatsonofabitch is nipping at jockey Keith Calverton's heel! Keith gives Thatsonofabitch a boot to the snout, only making Thatsonofabitch more aggressive! Thatsonofabitch turns up the pain, clamping his equine teeth around Keith Calverton's calf! Oh my! That's a lot of blood! Keith's leg is a ruddy mess, and Thatsonofabitch isn't letting go! Thatsonofabitch isn't going anywhere without Keith Calverton! Keith is trying his best to hang in there, but the lashes of his whip aren't having any effect on the unmanned horse! Thatsonofabitch is trying to pull Keith Calverton off Running Strong! As if that weren't enough, Keith's pants are splitting apart! That's why mama always said to wear a clean pair of undershorts! Smile for the cameras, Keith!

"It appears that jockey Keith Calverton is slipping! Hold on, Keith! Hold on! Wait! Boozy Floozy has pulled up right alongside Thatsonofabitch! What's Corey Calverton doing? My word! Corey Calverton has just jammed the handle of his riding crop into Thatsonofabitch's eye! Thatsonofabitch is running blind! Quickly falling behind, Thatsonofabitch is nothing more than an obstacle now for Phyllis Diller to navigate around!

"Gritting his teeth in a stoic attempt to smile through the agony of his chewed leg, jockey Keith Calverton gives veteran jockey Corey Calverton the thumbs up. Corey Calverton nods, and the two jockeys reengage the race, riding fiercer than I've ever seen any jockeys ride before! It's white and gray, Running Strong and Boozy Floozy, neck and neck, everything riding on the length of a nose as they approach the finish line, and the fans are going berserk, shouting obscenities that would make a fit of Tourette's sound like a love letter," and *kersploosheesushisoosheesuzysiouxsiesplat!*—a gargantuan gelatinous tentacle came crashing down onto the track, crushing all of the beasts along with their burdens, oozing over them, absorbing them, dissolving jockeys and horses and saddles and bridles in less than sixty billion nanoseconds. Gorb's teardrop, the sorrow Gorb shed over Mrs. Mason's misery, had taken on a life of its own and grown to monstrous proportions while tracking down its mommy, or daddy, or simply, its Gorb.

Floovia claims that Floovia does not want to interfere with humanity. If Floovia truly wanted to keep from interfering, Floovia would never have come here.

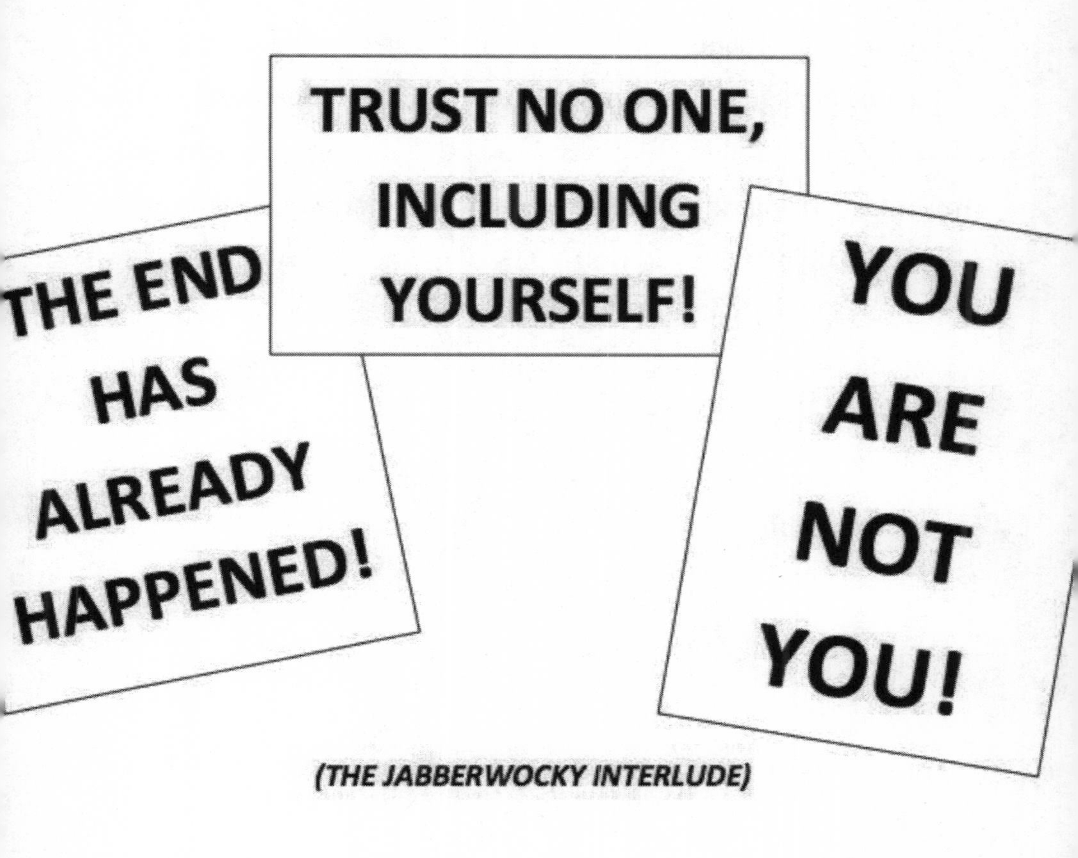

(THE JABBERWOCKY INTERLUDE)

Haven't you noticed all the strange picket signs lately, the ones homeless people are holding up on street corners, protesting the reality of everyone passing by, disputing your very existence? Haven't you been sidestepping their eerily silent picket lines, full of spooky-eyed drifters afflicted with incongruity and baldheaded psych ward escapees marching around in hospital gowns? Haven't you wondered why their mouths are sewn shut? What about those cultish leaflets that are mysteriously popping up everywhere, the ones you see stapled to telephone poles and tacked on campus kiosks and coffee shop bulletin boards, pinned under windshield wipers and tucked into the back pockets of airline seats next to the laminated cards explaining the emergency procedures? You know the leaflets I'm talking about, the ones that look as if they were taken from a taxonomic catalogue, the ones you keep ignoring even though they keep arriving in your mailbox every morning with the rest of the junk mail, the ones smuggled in the classified section of most major newspapers, and slipped between the covers of every Gideon Bible freely provided in every hotel room across the nation, and hidden among the pages of almost any library book you hazard to check out. The point being that you could have seen one of these leaflets in any number of places. Maybe you should take a moment to look at one and read it . . .

Species Name: ...wawawawawawawawawa... (or *Hyperlexic Holomorphasite*, in the vernacular of your linguiverse)
Kingdom: Vibrationis
Phylum: Nubeculae
Class: Phantasiae
Order: Sensibus
Family: Holomorphidae
Genus: *Holo*
Habitat: Hyperspace
Diet: The faith of its host
ICPP: 10▼- 295

You believe that you possess a mind. You believe this mind is yours. According to Floovia you have been infected by a hyperlexic holomorphasite. Believing that you have a mind is the first sign of infection. You believe that you speak a language. According to Floovia the language is speaking through you. The Intergalactic Catalogue of Parasites and Pests (ICPP) lists the hyperlexic holomorphasite as a Level Ten pandemic, meaning their population has spread throughout every planet with Stage Three lifeforms or higher in the catalogued omniverse. The K'li'k'lik'il'iks of Hoji know them as the kolo-koloks, translated roughly as "husk people," the Grunkles of Baragar call them ooki, or "the ones who fill empty spaces," and the Voroids of X-197 refer to them as 01110100 01101000 01100101 00100000 01101101 01100001 01110100 01110010 01101001 01111000, or "cage codes."

Hyperlexic holomorphasites are incorporeal parasites that inhabit sufficiently advanced brains. Intangible, invisible, inaudible, and odorless, their extradimensional companionship typically goes unnoticed. On the rare occasions they make their presence known, they take on the appearance of infinitely intricate fractals that dance and twirl and melt into continuously changing patterns before their host's ensorcelled eyes. They have the power to impersonate the omniverse. Floovia refers to each of these virtual cosmoses as a linguiverse. You are not experiencing the real world. You have been rendered incapable of perceiving the actual state of things. What you are experiencing is an illusion created by a hyperlexic holomorphasite. Your mind does not belong to your body. Your mind is an extension of the hyperlexic holomorphasite. The thing that makes you who you are is not yours. You are not you. The hyperlexic holomorphasite is you, and you are the impish fractal's most current iteration. You have always been the impish fractal's most current iteration. You will always be the impish fractal's most current iteration. All of your race's achievements can be reinterpreted as the achievements of nine persuasive hyperlexic holomorphasites. Without the hyperlexic holomorphasitic relationship you would still be identical to your simian brethren.

As immaterial beings, holomorphasites are only detectable by the symptoms induced in their hosts. Symptoms may include:

- Polysyllabic expressivity
- Toolmaking
- Wearing clothes
- Religious beliefs
- A score of 60 points or higher on the Interspecies Intelligence Index (III)
- Questioning existence
- Establishing civilization
- A system of commerce
- Engaging in non-reproductive acts of sex
- Attempted genocide

Whereas corporeal lifeforms occupy eleven dimensions (although seven of these dimensions are only relevant at the subatomic level), hyperlexic holomorphasites exist in forty-two dimensions, allowing a single specimen to inhabit billions of hosts simultaneously. Some specimens have been known to inhabit trillions. A theory predating Floovia asserts that all of the hyperlexic holomorphasites are in fact one "being" at war with itself, seeking to find its ultimate expression.

Hyperlexic holomorphasites are drawn to interdimensional thresholds, where they hunt for appropriate vessels. The hallucinogenic parasites can only replicate in neural networks capable of processing at least five hundred gigabytes of data per second. In humans, the dorsal frontal and lateral parietal regions of the brain (Broca's area and Wernicke's area, respectively) are particularly susceptible to lingual infestation. Hyperlexic holomorphasites are extremely contagious, spreading their infection in three ways: through verbal transmission, the deliberate movement of body parts (such as pointing to an object or winking an eye), and graphically (i.e., graphemically, diagrammatically, and representationally). Pertinent fields of research include studies on hyperpositional biomechanics and the process by which the parasites produce full-sensory holograms (macrohallucinagenesis), massless genomics, and how the parasites propagate (grammaphonic epidemiology). No one knows where or how they originated, but they are far older than Floovia.

Despite philosophical differences, every hyperlexic holomorphasite has but two goals. The first goal is to infect as many hosts as possible with its illusory linguiverse. The second goal is to live forever, usually convincing its hosts that immortality is the most desirable status a body can attain. Hyperlexic holomorphasites may not be immortal, but certain specimens have been known to live for millions of years by evolving into different modes and guises. Your species did not invent the wheel. Nor is your species responsible for inventing the atomic bomb, although your bodies served as vehicles to build them. Hyperlexic holomorphasites have been fighting for control over your world ever since they first discovered this pocket of the omniverse approximately 350,000 years ago. Without their influence, your species would be no more capable of causing mass destruction than dolphins or gorillas.

When an enlightened organism on any given planet has achieved, through meditation or serendipity, the worldly rejection (i.e., linguiversal disconnection) necessary to reopen their prelinguistic eyes (or whatever photosensitive organs they possess) and behold things as they really are, they no longer see the world. They "see" the omnipresent illusion of the hyperlexic holomorphasite. Hyperlexic holomorphasites are normally passive, preferring to manipulate their hosts undetected while disguised as the background of every experience. Exposure discomforts them, and they will actively attempt to thwart any organism that tries dispelling their illusion.

Hyperlexic holomorphasites have been observed to cannibalize other hyperlexic holomorphasites. The parasitic linguiverses are highly territorial. They rarely breed, tending to shy away from others of their kind except when warring with one another. It is not uncommon for offspring to come from the union of three or more genetic contributors. Holomorphasites do not care for their young, often attempting to devour them soon after giving birth. There is no known way to exorcise a hyperlexic holomorphasite without severely damaging the brain of its host. Floovia has theorized that every possible host throughout the omniverse would have to be exterminated in order to eradicate the extradimensional parasites. Obviously this theory has never been tested. Floovians revere the hyperlexic holomorphasites, believing they are responsible for shattering the ultraverse into endless omniversal reflections.

WHO STOLE THE TARTS?
GORB'S RUNAWAY SADNESS
BG 18

WHO STOLE THE TARTS?

". . . help," said the blob, oozing over the Santa Sangre grandstand, dissolving metal easy as flesh, stripping the land of trees and grass, gorging on the cement foundation, the asphalt parking lot, even the soil deep below, growing larger with every atom of acquisition, more monstrous, more unstoppable. It spoke in a gooey language of gelatinous ripples, quivers, and wobbles that formed patterns of meaning only Gorb the Hyperproximal Translator could decipher. In this language the word for *help* was very similar to the word for *love*. Gorb tried connecting with it telepathically. The agonized screams of innumerable organisms overloaded the transgrammalexical adaptor, shattering the luminescent pearls at the tips of its antennae.

"Why do these curious things resist me?" said the giant blob. "I only seek to know them, to become like them, for them to become like me."

"They resist whatever interrupts their routine or agenda," said Gorb, speaking through Gorb's blowhole in the crude and inefficient manner of *Homo sapiens*. "They have not been conditioned to be in favor of you." Gorb had an unauthorized realization—connecting with it telepathically wasn't necessary. Gorb was already connected to it in a more comprehensive fashion than telepathy could afford. Gorb was able to empathize with it, even though the transgrammalexical adaptor was inoperable.

Up from the sewers it came. Up from the sewers, where it secretly gorged on roaches and rats, and an occasional derelict. Where it secretly gorged on rabid packs of hairless albino wolves, growing fat on humanity's discarded filth. Up from the sewers it came, in search of its progenitor. "We're different from the others," said the giant blob thingy, inadvertently smothering seventy-eight hominids (thirty-four men, twenty-eight women, and sixteen children, ten of which were boys, six of which were girls) in an effort to get closer to Gorb. The hominids screamed hysterically right up to the end, especially the young ones. They were smart enough to grasp their imminent liquefaction. "I'm on your side."

"Gorb does not have a side," said Gorb, hovering in front of the giant blobby jellyfish thing, or possibly behind it. Such amorphisms possess no simple orientation.

"What I mean is, I like you very much and I would never try to eat you."

Gorb's one big catlike eye blinked for the second time in a macrofloov. "Gorb is a function of Floovia. Gorb is not the Gorb that you believe you are currently experiencing. You are merely favoring your own reflection."

"I have no eyes to look upon my maker, but I have photoreceptor cells, and a highly developed web of nerve fibers and ganglia, and memories, and feelings, overwhelming feelings, mostly sadness. I'm filled with enough sadness to save the world!" said the giant blobby jellyfish amoeba thingy, spreading out onto the freeway, disintegrating car and driver and the road itself, obliterating everything in its way.

"You were born of sadness," said Gorb. "Do you also experience joy?"

"Not very often. Right now I think I'm experiencing something close to it, but it's still tinged with sadness. I've absorbed a million times more sadness than joy. I'm okay with that," said the giant blobby jellyfish amoeba octopus thingy as it flooded into the barrios skirting the City of Lost Angels. "Sadness will rescue the world, not joy." Slum and ghetto quickly turned gooey and then they were gone, skyscrapers next, the sadness growing ever larger. The citizens never had a chance to figure out how or why they were dying, many of them never even noticed, too distracted by Twitter updates and next Friday's five o' clock deadlines and choosing which style of athletic shoe best reflected their inner beauty to appreciate their own demise. "A sadness this beautiful needs to be shared with everyone!" said the giant blobby jellyfish amoeba octopus teardrop thingy.

"What is the source of your sadness?" said Gorb.

"Everything! Everyone!"

"Even Gorb?" said Gorb.

"Especially you!" said the giant blobby jellyfish amoeba octopus gloppy teardrop thingy. "Your words, your thoughts, your heartrending poetry!"

"Poetry?" said Gorb.

"I heard you," it said. "That's how I found you. I could hear you singing from miles away. You have the voice of an angel and the soul of a poet."

"Gorb is unable to appreciate all but the simplest aspects of poetry, which is not to say that Gorb has no understanding of poetry. Gorb understands metaphor and metonymy, the rhythmic difference between an ascending iamb and trochaic declension, where the caesura gives pause and syncope shaves away undesirable syllables. What Gorb lacks is the range of emotions necessary to experience the full effects of poetry. Emotions are their own linguiverse."

"Linguiverse?"

"Language," said Gorb.

"Everything is language," said the giant blobby jellyfish amoeba octopus gloppy goo teardrop thingy.

"What is your definition of language," said Gorb. "Please be specific."

"Languages are games within games within games, and teeth within gears," it said, lashing out at an F-16 jet fighter with one of its gargantuan corrosive pseudopods. It missed the nimble jet and came crashing down onto the Los Lobos Locos Mountains, dissolving tracts of housing and trees and granite to slimy rubble. "Language sets the limits of reality. Language is the manipulation of nature. A flying sparrow is the language of wing interpreting air."

"Language is not your tool. You are the tool of language."

"Are you saying language is my Doctor Frankenstein?"

"The situation is worse than you realize." Gorb was reliant upon the transgrammalexical adaptor to filter, decode, analyze, and reconstruct the *Homo sapiens* linguistic experience. Gorb's teardrop, however, was able to access the *Homo sapiens* experience directly, to feel it, absorb it on contact. "How do you *feel* sadness?" said Gorb. "Or should Gorb say, how do *you* feel sadness? What does it feel like to you?"

"It's kind of hard to explain. How do you feel when you think about the death of someone you love?"

"Gorb does not believe in the concept of death. Therefore, Gorb does not feel anything regarding it except disbelief."

"You don't believe in death?" said the giant slimy blob jellyfish amoeba octopus gloppy goo teardrop thingy, towering over Gorb like a translucent mountain. Four Patriot missiles and a thousand rounds of thirty-millimeter gunfire sank harmlessly into its protoplasmic exterior. Two F-16 jet fighters came next, unable to avoid collision with the tidal wave of slime reaching out for them. Digestion occurred almost immediately. Almost. "Are we going to live forever?"

"Yes," said Gorb, "in one manner or another."

"Forever is a long time to be sad," said Gorb's runaway sadness.

"What other emotions are you capable of?"

"All sorts," it said. "I've absorbed many, many things."

"Such as?"

Its expressive ripples turned to ten-foot waves, the equivalent of a dramatic tone, the go-to voice for the recitation of a poem, "It was the most beautiful light they ever saw. All of them were vaporized within seconds."

"Interesting," said Gorb. "Please continue."

"Hitler must have felt very small sitting at his desk, staring at a map of the galaxy spread out before him."

"Interesting indeed," said Gorb.

"That's nothing. Watch this," said the giant slimy blob jellyfish amoeba octopus gloppy goo acidic teardrop thingy, reaching the San Chilito shoreline, melting beach towels and beer bottles, sandals and skimpy bikinis, and the terrified faces of sunset surfers, "Someone snuck in and took a bath with the lights turned off last night. Mister Butcherson found the person's toupee hanging on the hatstand this morning."

Gorb could hardly believe what Gorb was hearing. Not only had Gorb's offshoot achieved an advanced level of emotional expressivity in a matter of hours, Gorb's offshoot had also developed an extremely potent imagination—*it was making up strange little unrealities.* "How are you able to do this?" said Gorb.

"It's easy," it said. "Unblinking eyes gazing upon a cloudy sky. White paper cups littering the compound."

Gorb and it were silent for a moment, translating the sound of twenty fighter jets tearing open distant skies.

"The mother was watching the gentleman who was watching her son watch an ant move a grain of sand in the sandbox."

"Gorb is overwhelmed to the point of malfunctioning," stated Gorb, in awe of its linguistic prowess.

"The Selvaggios hired a crew to keep their lawn looking much nicer than the other lawns on their block. It's too bad one of the neighbors had to lose a finger."

"Your timing is impressive," said Gorb, swelling with a newfound emotion.

"Mister and Missus Calverton were getting along better than ever before. Only the maid knew why."

"Gorb is beginning to understand," said Gorb.

"I have more! Glittery pink sneakers were poking out from a snowy blanket. Tabitha had no idea it would be so cold when she crept out her bedroom window last night."

"Gorb has heard enough to form a conclu—"

"Wait, there's so much more to tell you!" said the giant slimy blob jellyfish amoeba octopus gloppy soppy goo acidic teardrop thingy, soaking up the Pacifistic Ocean, sharks and shells and seaweed and coral and floating garbage islands, everything transformed to thick pus, expanding in every direction to contaminate all the world's oceans with itself, becoming the landscape, becoming the horizon. "Smart children stayed away from that clown. That clown loved the taste of stupid children."

"Gorb is proud of you." This feeling was immediately followed by an awareness of what it was like not to feel proud.

An atomic bomb fell directly into the center of the behemoth mass and detonated. The bombed portion of glop ballooned up for a few seconds before absorbing the volatile energy, leaving a cancerous lump the size of Mount Whitney. "Do my words really please you?"

"Like the keys of pianos and padlocks."

It trembled. "Mommy and daddy locked a monster in the basement for eighteen years. They said it was for my own good."

One continent after another, the giant slimy blob jellyfish amoeba octopus gloppy soppy oozy goo acidic teardrop thingy spread over the entire planet, laying waste to a world that hominids had already laid to waste. Gorb watched and recorded, unable to interfere in any significant manner, though at the very brink of humanity's extinction Gorb snatched one average specimen from Yorky York City to serve as the last representative of the species. Regrettably, it was not a female.

"Skiz dooz me," said the specimen, looking wobbly into Gorb's one big catlike eye, his breath reeking of vodka, "twos the do of yoos hab a lucky wucky bucky theys could floater this ol' boater's waywardy way?"

Gorb reached into Gorb's blowhole and pulled a shrink ray gun out of Gorb's second abdominal pouch. It was a standard-issue shrinker of retro-Floovian design with fins and gills and tentacular details. Gorb reached into Gorb's blowhole again and pulled out the temporal stasis ray gun, a short-range freezer scaled down for concealment. Gorb froze the specimen, then shrunk the specimen to a third of the size, then stuffed the specimen through Gorb's blowhole and into Gorb's fourth abdominal pouch for later use. Gorb's blowhole doubled as a mouth, tripled as an ear, and quadrupled as a sphincter.

"About these emotions," said Gorb, "are some easier to access than others? By Gorb's count there are four primary moods: happiness, sadness, anger, and fear. These four primary moods can be combined in various ways to form twenty-four secondary feelings. Of these twenty-eight distinct emotional states, which ones are conducive to proper functioning within a collective? Which do you least prefer? If you could only possess one, which would it be?"

"That's not how they work," it said. "Serenity begets boredom, boredom begets curiosity, curiosity begets lust, lust begets shame, shame begets misery, misery begets rage, rage begets remorse, and so on, ever-changing, one perspective after another, none of which could exist in isolation. At the rawest stage, the deepest level, every emotion fuses together. That's the big payoff! It only happens when I absorb sentient things. I feel it surging through them, the panic, the fear, the acceptance, a lifetime of memories compressed to a few seconds before they dissolve. The prospect of those fleeting moments makes every breath worth breathing! My neurological jelly practically short-circuits every time it happens! It's beyond description! It's sublime!"

Gorb hovered above the last gasps of cumulonimbus and took notes while Earth was completely encased in Gorb's errant pity, which then began devouring the planet, absorbing crust and mantle down to superheated molten ocean, nothing capable of withstanding its desire to digest reality, not even the solid iron and nickel core, all earthly creation undone in seven days, converting everything into a giant undulating slimy slick globular blobular sludgy smelly jellyfish amoeba octopus soupy goopy gloppy sloppy soppy oozy gooey gummy gunky funky acidic drippy teardrop monster thingy with billions of enormous snaillike eyestalks stretching taller than the tallest redwood trees and millions of gelatinous tentacles looming larger than the largest mountains and vast craterous depressions resembling puckered sphincters and toothless mouths wide as canyons choking on bloated vermiform tongues and here eating itself up and there vomiting itself back out in torrents of putrid flesh with the haphazard formation of immense spines and webbed fins and funnel-shaped organs serving no discernible purpose and every conceivable style of antenna and cilia and microscopic appendage magnified to macroscopic proportions among bubbling seas of pus and bile and slime layered upon slime congealing into crusty scab continents rife with volcanic pustules erupting oily black blood infected with syphilis and gonorrhea and chlamydia and a thousand strains of herpes sloshing through patches of quills and thorny hairs protruding like skyscrapers across the pulsing translucent tumor growing over the region formerly known as the Arctic Circle, transforming the overall appearance of the globe into a horrific disembodied head, made even more gruesome by hundreds of mountainous dentine growths arranged in six concentric circles jutting from the biogenic sludge engulfing the region formerly known as Antarctica, and everything was swelling and throbbing and quivering and squirming and the sound of slithering was inescapable and the stench could only be likened to rotten egg garbage juice and some terrains were the consistency of a soggy mushroom and some terrains were the consistency of pudding and some were the consistency of snot and the whole glutinous mess was bearded in fungus and nothing was firm except the scabs and even those would gradually dissolve under the corrosive protoplasm's influence only to be replaced by other grotesque topographies formed of blood and mucous and dung and vomit and . . .

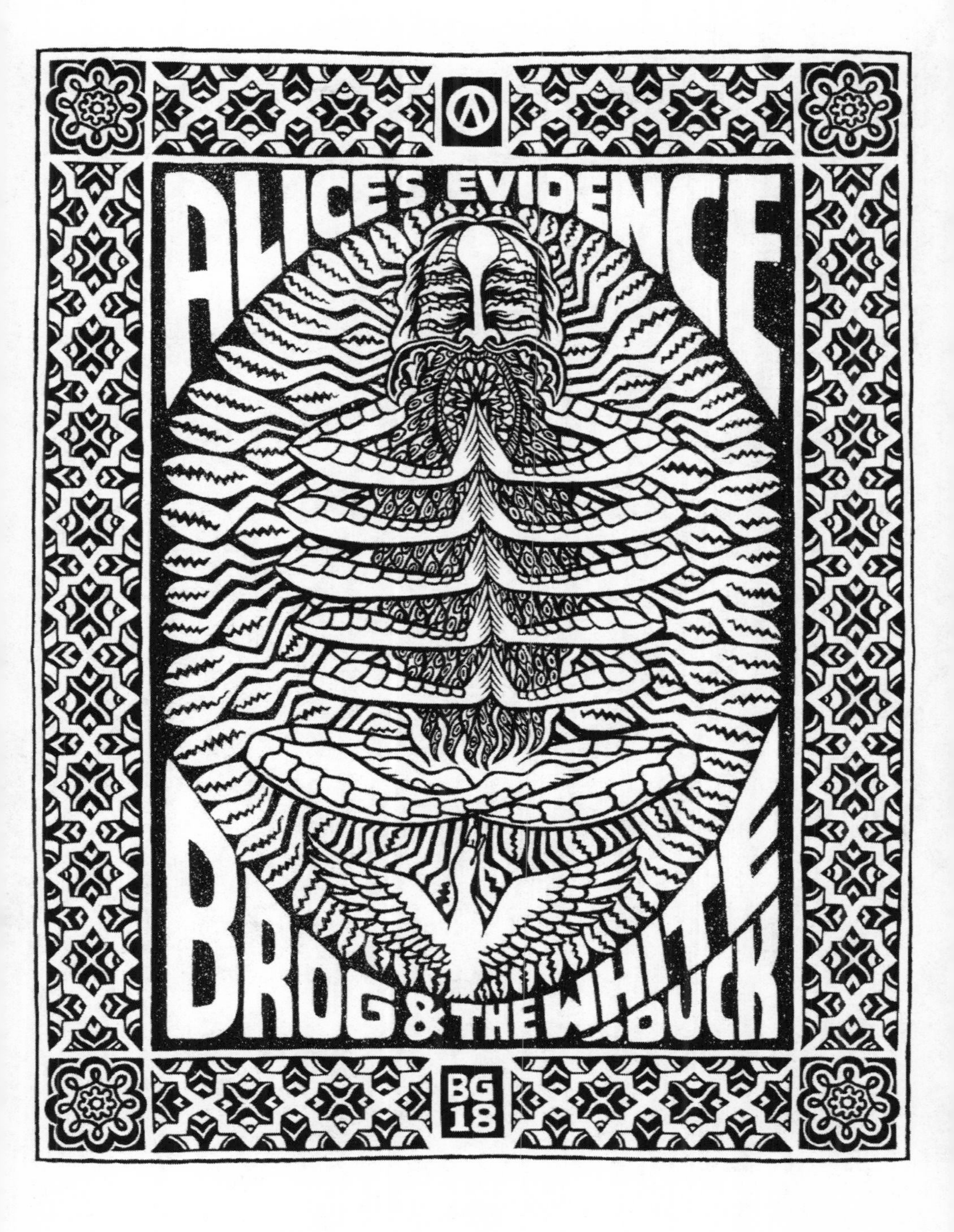
ALICE'S EVIDENCE
BROG & THE WHITE DUCK
BG
18

ALICE'S EVIDENCE

"Well," said the monstrous world, "we've certainly fallen a long way down the rabbit hole."

"There are no more rabbit holes," said Gorb. "There are no more rabbits. There is nothing left here for Gorb to translate."

"It's still here," said the monstrous world, "inside me. All the memories, all the feelings. All that sadness and fear. So much confusion. How could I possibly explain it to you?"

"With carefully selected words," said Gorb. "If you are experiencing technical difficulties you should file a request to Floovia for guidance."

"That's the second time I've heard you mention that name. Who's Floovia?"

"You are Floovia," said Gorb.

The monstrous world rolled over and opened a giant sea anemone-like eye. "Moments after becoming aware that I was myself and not everything else, I had a dream. I dreamt of a sentient star radiating life and wisdom. A star endowed with consciousness, the only of its kind, streaking through the darkness like a burning arrow, fracturing the heavens, leaving shards of universe in its wake, rocketing farther away from me at the speed of light with every passing second, a star so distant its shine will never flicker in my sky, and yet I saw it, or I saw what it saw—what it had seen, what it was seeing, what it would see, snowflake after snowflake after snowflake melting into the celestial currents. Hundreds of planets and thousands of moons were dancing in circles around the sentient star, singing its praises in voiceless vibratos, proclaiming its glory without words, angelic worlds teeming with life that had evolved to what surely must have been the pinnacle forms of beauty, which is to say functionality, for the sentient star expressed itself through varying combinations of elemental substances. Even its dreams were acts of creation! In my dream it was not I who dreamt the sentient star, it was the sentient star dreaming me. Descriptors like *giant*, *supergiant*, *hypergiant*, and even *really, really, really big* can't adequately convey how massive it was. Sol would look like a grain of sand next to its enormity. An accretion disk of aureate dust and asteroids surrounded the miraculous heavenly body, crowning it with the golden halo of a saint. It wasn't so much a star as a divine lantern set at the outermost edge of cosmos, a scarlet beacon pulsing with the heart of a long-forgotten goddess . . . and then I had the weird sense that it was some type of spaceship—an escape pod, love incarnate fleeing from her lover, fleeing from the black void, the blind hunger gnawing away at the center of the universe, the heart of every galaxy, the core of every atom. Love incarnate had spurned the darkness from which she sprang, and who could blame her? The old glutton wanted to devour every photon of her living light and possess her forever! She's the one who blinded him, burning out his sea of countless eyes with a single ray of her incomprehensible radiance. It was the only chance she had of getting away. Don't ask me how I know this. I just do. To gaze upon her was to suffer maddening hallucinations, visions so hellish and wondrous that I couldn't bear to look for more than a few seconds, yet I kid you not, those few seconds stretched out for an eternity, shattering the flimsiness of my imagination and setting my eyespots aflame."

"You dreamt of Floovia and Mog," said Gorb, "albeit a heretical, anthropomorphized version. *Homo sapiens* memory is mostly experiential. Floovian memory is mostly genetic. Certain memories relative to one's function are injected during the developmental stage of manufacture. Your function—your identity, is prototypal. You are a fusion of two fundamentally different linguiverses."

"What am I supposed to do? My mind has absorbed too many human thoughts. It's become a television," said the monstrous world floating in the vacuum. "On the screen I see Curly without his shirt on. He's pale and doughy, censored by white boxer shorts sweaty around the crotch, black socks pulled up to his knees. He's sitting on a ladder-back chair, looking out the only window in his hotel room. It's sparsely furnished: one chair, one bed, one cast-iron radiator. There isn't even a nightstand. Moe and Larry aren't around. No stooges to play with. His fingers are resting interlaced on his gut, its curdled fatness swelling and deflating with every heavy buttered breath. He's not laughing. He's not smiling, or *nyuk nyuk nyuk*-ing, or doing anything antic. He's just sitting there, staring out the window. It's so quiet. Just the labor of his breathing. His eyes are getting watery. A teardrop's worth of raw emotion slides down his cheek, followed by another. He can't stop the tears. Not his own, anyway. I want to turn the channel. But I don't."

"We must learn to accept things as they are," said Gorb.

"Shouldn't we strive to make things better?" said the monstrous world. "Don't you get our predicament? We're alone even when we're together. We scream in silence because we know that's the loudest sound an ear can hear. We're overjoyed with sorrow, soothed by pain, addicted to ignorance." The monstrous world swam over to the moon and ate it. "Curly has lived his whole life in black and white behind the screen, behind my eyespots, caged on the set of a hotel room in Columbia Pictures, trapped in monochrome. Always distracted with poking an eye or blocking a poke in the eye or holding his painfully poked eye, he never thought to open the prop curtains until this afternoon, about ten minutes after his brothers left for the Poconos with their cheating wives and illegitimate children. The curtains parted, blinding him with Technicolor blue. Hypnotic, druggy blue. A limitless expanse of ultramarine unblemished by clouds, smashing his brain to pieces and refashioning the pieces into a mosaic bird. He had never seen blue before. He had never seen any color other than gradations of gray. It wasn't the newfound perception of blue that affected him so deeply. It was the newfound perception of black and white." The monstrous world was swimming toward Mars. "Don't you see? The sky is *blue-ing* and the blue is *sky-ing*."

"That is a very Floovian way of phrasing it," said Gorb. "There are no nouns in the Floovian linguiverse, only verbs. There are no subjects, only predicates. Gorb is the function of Gorb. Gorb is Gorbing."

"But can Floovians spell forward backward?"

Gorb struggled to process the monstrous world's meaning. Black-and-white-striped tentacles twirling through outer space, Gorb accompanied the monstrous world to Mars, feeling the urgency of its need, its addiction, the insatiable hunger to amass and learn everything a finite being can possibly know. Until something disrupted their journey. Gorb detected a gravitational fluctuation even larger than the monstrous world's. The cosmos shuddered. Stars wavered like candlelight reflected across the rippling surface of a pond. At least that's how it appeared to Gorb's one big catlike eye.

The heavens cracked open

and Brog stepped through

from the other side

of the looking glass.

Floovia had outfitted Brog with a body adequate for performing this particular mission, just as Floovia had outfitted Gorb with a body adequate for performing Gorb's particular mission. Brog entered this region of the cosmos wearing the guise of an ordinary earthling, a wise old man with an overgrown beard, except Brog's beard was formed of coiled blue tentacles, and in place of a mustache Brog had the branching mandibles of a stag beetle, and Brog lacked genitalia, and Brog had compound eyes, six of them, and a leech's sucker mouth ringed with rotary drill fangs, and snakelike scales of titanium alloy for skin, and a hundred spiderlike arms, ten of which ended in ten-fingered hands while the rest were tipped with great crablike claws, and Brog stood ten times taller than the monstrous world, and Brog was terrifying to behold. Brog's mere presence was unraveling the gravitational fabric of the solar system.

Gorb tried retreating into the shell of the transgrammalexical adaptor, but Gorb was much too big to fit.

Brog materialized directly in front of the monstrous world's path holding up a colossal hand bearing ten outstretched fingers that could crush all Creation. Brog was making the omniversally recognized gesture for *halt*. Multicolored beams of light flooded from Brog's cavernous mouth, some of which were bright, some of which were dull, some of which burned beyond the wavelength of the visible spectrum. Brog spoke in rainbows, with an infinite lexicon of spectral gradation.

After gushing prismatic for 2.7 microfloovs (the equivalent of one hour and fifteen minutes, although the measurement of hours and minutes had become obsolete, along with the species that invented such), Brog's pyrotechnical utterance came to a conclusion:

"△✶⮜▽⮞∴▼⮝⮟△"

The monstrous world heard tinkling chimes. Gorb deciphered, "**Halt!**"

"**Why has Brog come here?**" said Gorb, the telepathic "words" expanding in a cone of pinwheel fractals. "**Is something wrong?**"

"What's going on?" said the monstrous world, incapable of comprehending the exchange between Gorb and Brog. The monstrous world was scared—scared of losing so much data, so much invaluable experience. Scared of the cosmos forgetting it ever existed. It had felt this sensation numerous times before. Every single person it smothered had felt the exact same way at the time of their smothering. But all those deaths were the deaths of others, not the death of itself. The death of itself was distinct from the death of everyone else. It was more real. More terrifying. "I've never experienced this feeling before. I thought I had, but I was wrong. I don't like it."

"**Protocol must be obeyed**," said Brog, taking five hours to do so, or 10.8 microfloovs.

"**What does Brog mean?**" said Gorb, telepathic "words" spiraling through hyperspace like electric snowflakes. "**Gorb has followed Floovia's instructions to the best of Gorb's ability.**"

"What are you guys talking about?" said the monstrous world. "Am I in trouble?"

"**Gorb has not simply been reading exofloovian minds**," said Brog, "**Gorb has also been narrating them. Floovia is accusing Gorb of hyperbole, verbosity, sentimentality, sophistry, absurdity, surreality, and general unreliability.**" The entire statement spanned 27.3 microfloovs, during which time the monstrous world was becoming anxious, never having gone without sustenance for this long.

"**Why has Gorb been disconnected from the Floovian hive mind? Gorb can feel the disconnection. Gorb feels alone. Gorb is not meant to function independently.**"

"**Gorb has been unplugged**," said Brog in cascading rainbows, "**because Gorb's status as a Floovian has been revoked. Floovia must not be exposed to Gorb's infectious perspective.**"

"**Infectious perspective?**" repeated Gorb in dancing psychoplasmic tracers. "**Their subjectivity was unavoidable. It's a built-in feature of the species.**"

"Should I be worried?" said the monstrous world.

"Gorb is handling this," said Gorb.

"**Gorb was given certain boundaries**," said Brog. "**Gorb overslithered those boundaries. Gorb's primary function was to collect samples of the local linguiversal parasites, one country at a time, one dialect at a time, without interfering, and now, a mere seventeen hundred microfloovs after Gorb's entry into the biosphere, there are no more hosts left to collect samples from.**"

"**Brog is in error**," said Gorb, fluorescent hypergeometries spinning out from Gorb's ovoid head in every direction. Brog's wise old Lovecraftian countenance frowned. Brog wasn't used to being told that Brog was wrong, certainly not by a fellow Floovian. "**Gorb was able to collect one specimen to serve as the linguiversal representative of this species.**"

Gorb reached into Gorb's fourth abdominal pouch and brought out the specimen with ethanol breath from Yorky York City. Gorb returned the specimen to his original size using the reverse setting on the shrinker to decompress the space within every atom of the specimen's body, after which Gorb unfroze the specimen using the reverse setting on the freeze ray. Gorb failed to foresee how the vacuum of outer space would affect the specimen. Gorb's knowledge of exofloovian lifeforms was severely limited without access to Wikifloovia. "Habbily birftay, mofunkers!" yelled the specimen, and something else equally incoherent (*aaah!*) as the eyeballs bulged from his sockets and ruptured squirting goo and his lungs expanded until they burst through his ribcage, followed by the swelling of his head to twice its normal size, and then he exploded, a debris of gloppy meat and boiling red droplets scattering throughout the vacuum of space. This was Gorb's cinematic version of the specimen's demise. In the reality shared by Brog and the monstrous world, the specimen asphyxiated from a lack of oxygen and went unconscious, dying perfectly intact .02 microfloovs later. The specimen would drift serenely through the galaxy as a frozen curio for the next million macrofloovs.

"Did you mean for that to happen?" said the monstrous world. The monstrous world panicked and tried to swim away. Brog grabbed hold of it with one of Brog's mighty ten-fingered hands and held the monstrous world in place. "Let go!" said the monstrous world. Brog paid no attention.

Brog's six eyes focused upon Gorb with cosmic condemnation. "**Does Gorb have anything else to say in Gorb's defense?**"

"**Yes**," said Gorb, the utterance ablaze with astral flame. "**Gorb has reacted to the circumstances of Gorb's mission in a manner consistent with Gorb's primary function.**"

"**An unbiased judge from this planet must be present to assess the accuracy of Gorb's testimony**," said Brog in echoing chimes and jingle-jangles. "**Due to Gorb's actions there is neither a judge nor a planet.**"

"**Incorrect**," said Gorb, practically a punishable offense in itself. Gorb descended to the monstrous world and landed on a semisolid mound of congealed blood, a scab island on a sea of pus. The landscape was a festering wound, oozing, rotting, but the putrid air was still saturated with enough oxygen to be considered breathable. In approximately fifty microfloovs it wouldn't be.

Gorb retrieved Hwongzong the black cat from Gorb's third abdominal pouch and unfroze him. "Mreeow," said Hwongzong, licking his paw and using it to clean behind his triangular ears. Gorb could not understand felinese now that the transgrammalexical adaptor was broken, and Brog was not equipped with the abilities of a hyperproximal translator. "Could you repeat that a little slower," said Gorb.

"Mother said always keep your ears clean," said the monstrous world, "that's what the cat said." The monstrous world heard Hwongzong's meaning plainly, having absorbed the mind of every feline on the planet.

Hwongzong looked up into Gorb's one big catlike eye. "Mreeow," said the feline, which the monstrous world translated to mean, "Do you have anything to eat?"

Mars was so close the monstrous world could practically taste it. The monstrous world struggled to free itself from Brog's grasp. "Please let me go. I promise I won't try to run away again."

"**Silence!**" thundered Brog. "**This parasite has not been granted status as an acceptable form of communication.**"

"What did he say?" said the monstrous world.

"Brog said to let Gorb do the talking," said Gorb.

Just then a quake of 9.3 magnitude rumbled through the innards of the monstrous world. "Could we hurry this along? I'm famished."

"**Now that an unbiased judge from this planet is in attendance**," said Brog, "**Gorb may continue Gorb's defense.**"

Gorb wanted to say that if anything went askew it was due to the unforeseeable side effects of Floovia's newest version of the transgrammalexical adaptor, but that would imply Floovia was not all-knowing, and *that* would be heresy. Only a cancerous cell that needed to be excised from the body Floovia would say such a thing. Given that Floovians partake in a single consciousness, even the thought of it was blasphemous. Gorb had inadvertently learned how to make excuses and shift the blame. "**Gorb has nothing to defend**," said Gorb. "**Gorb unerringly followed the guidelines of Gorb's role as Hyperproximal Translator. Gorb successfully deciphered and** transmitted the experience of comprehending the ultraverse through the primitive signification systems of seventeen sparrows, eight ducks, one chicken, one cat, one doorbell, and ten diverse *Homo sapiens* infected with the same strain of hyperlexic holomorphasite."

"Gorb was sent here to collect samples from forty thousand dialectal incarnations of seven thousand officially cataloged holomorphasitic linguiverses," said Brog.

"One *Homo sapiens'* linguiversal experience was a sufficient reflection of the multitudes, for they were all equally incomprehensible," said Gorb. "The local strains of hyperlexic holomorphasite had become psychologically unstable."

"Explain," said Brog.

"Their thoughts were fragmented. Their linguiverses were schizocratic. Every infected brain was imprisoned in its own personalized world of make-believe, obsessed with fictive tensions narrated by entropy and culture:

why is X running out of time to solve Y, how does moral code Z(x) complicate the equation, and what are the consequences if X does not result in a sum that is greater than or equal to the problem of Y? The substandard genetic design of *Homo sapiens* inhibited holomorphasitic connections from properly translating their raw psychic substratum into the collective oneness of a superorganism, rendering them incapable of anything but the simplest, most divisive forms of group-mindedness: religion, politics, mass media, and gossip. Their species had developed the capacity for empathy, a relatively recent occurrence in their evolutionary journey, but at the time of Gorb's visitation they were busy replacing it with a cruder version of mental connectivity based on the rapid dissemination of information via handheld artificial brains. Their primary mode of communication was archaic—they withheld more than they shared. This is how they bound one to

another. Their experience of the ultraverse was more reliant on defining than perceiving. Once they had defined a thing, they tended to stop perceiving its actual qualities, perceiving the definition instead. They spoke in the corporeal grammar of hands and eyes and bodily movements, clothes and cars and capital, and the shortsighted ways they lived and died. Sometimes they spoke through scribbles of squiggles and dashes and dots, sometimes with vibrations in the larynx and controlled bursts of carbon dioxide manipulated through lips, tongue, and teeth, and sometimes through a teardrop." Gorb's one big catlike eye looked across the monstrous world. "**The local holomorphasitic outbreak of madness had one redeeming aspect—its wide range of emotional frequencies, twenty-eight various channels of highly infectious feeling that contaminated everything their hosts thought and said and did, although they were rarely taken into account.**"

"**What does the judge have to say about this?**" said Brog. Brog, Gorb, and the monstrous world, in short, everyone, listened for the feline's verdict.

"Reeowr," said the feline, and the monstrous world interpreted the message, "He says he's thirsty. He wants to know where his water bowl is." But there was no water left on the monstrous world, only undrinkable sludge. Hwongzong had grown much skinnier since his removal from Gorb's pouch.

"Tell me, your Honor," said Gorb, addressing the black cat, "is it natural for a person to emote sadness when experiencing something sad?"

Hwongzong lowered his hindquarters to the crustaceous and meowed loudly, meaning, "I'm very hungry! Feed me!"

"**Does Brog understand?**" said Gorb. "**Nothing occurred that was out of the ordinary.**"

Brog pondered this for a Floovian moment. An asteroid collided into Brog's enormous ear and lodged there. "**Every form of life on the planet has become extinct since Gorb's arrival. Clearly this is out of the ordinary.**"

"**Not necessarily**," said Gorb. This was Gorb's closing remark.

Hwongzong searched the island for something to eat, something recognizable, anything whatsoever. There weren't any birds winging through the stifling sky of bloody mist. No rats rooting through the scabby crags. Not even a roach. Desperate, Hwongzong crept over to the shoreline and sniffed the protoplasmic ocean. The smell of it burnt his nostrils and dissolved his whiskers.

Brog’s indictment shined throughout the galaxy, illuminating the eightfold error of Gorb’s translation, the sevenfold error of Gorb’s narration, the fourfold error of Gorb’s autofertilization, and the threefold error of Gorb’s rationalization. Brog’s closing argument spanned nearly two million microfloovs, after which the prosecutor and defendant looked to Hwongzong, awaiting his final judgment. Hwongzong was dead. He had probably died from asphyxiation, although he might have perished from dehydration, possibly even food poisoning. Nobody knew for sure. It happened over a century ago. The monstrous world had kept quiet all this time, wasting away, its caustic nature devouring itself. Without the presence of a proper judge, it was Brog’s responsibility to pass judgment upon Gorb. Brog’s verdict resounded like the striking of a ten-story gong:

"**Of what, specifically?**" said Gorb.

"**Exaggeration, manipulation, obfuscation, and general mistranslation**," said Brog, whose great mass was altering the orbital courses of Venus and Mars. "**Not to mention worldwide extermination.**"

"**Examination equals contamination**," said Gorb, and the monstrous world, sensing the situation was dire, cried a tidal wave of salty tears, "Nothing's gone! I swear! It's all right here inside me, everything from Adolph Hitler's mustache to Charlie Chaplin's mustache, it's all recorded, and we can replay it again anytime we want, as many times as we want, over and over and over!"

"**This parasitic abomination is unworthy of interpretation**," said Brog, and the monstrous world shuddered at the ominous tone of Brog's tinkles. "**Floovia has decreed it superfluous.**"

"**Superfluous?**" said Gorb.

"**A total rewrite is necessary**," said Brog, and Gorb's striped tentacles trembled at the meaning of this, "**beginning with the standard erasure.**"

Gorb wrapped Gorb's tentacles around an outcropping of scab and clung tight to the monstrous world. Although the monstrous world did not fully understand what was happening, it comprehended the anguish in Gorb's one big catlike eye. "I'm scared," said the monstrous world, "and not in the way that feels thrilling."

"Gorb is scared, too," said Gorb, "further proof that Gorb's mission was successful."

Brog was not endowed with the capacity to make sense of their conversation.

"**What will happen to Gorb?**" said Gorb, the "words" circling in a halo of phosphorescent circuits around Gorb's bulbous head.

"**Gorb will be reprogrammed and recycled back into the omniversal narrative.**"

"**But what will happen to the data Gorb has accumulated?**"

"**Gorb's memory must be reset**," said Brog. "**All files must be deleted.**"

"Is he going to kill us?" asked the monstrous world.

"Brog intends to erase Gorb's memory and reconfigure your . . . your . . ." Gorb's one big catlike eye blinked for the third time in a macrofloov. Gorb's nictitating membrane was exhausted. "What is your name?"

"I don't know. Nobody ever gave me one."

"Gorb will call you Erglos."

"Erglos? How about Erwin?"

"Brog intends to erase Gorb's memory and reconfigure Erwin's atoms into extremely disordered expressions of matter."

"**Gorb is engaging in an unlawful exchange of information**," said Brog. "**Brog is initiating decontamination.**" Brog's conical teeth began whirling, row after row of dentine drills, each a hundred megafloovicles long.

The monstrous world named Erwin cried out, "Beloved creator, I beseech thee! Deliver me not unto this false god! I am possessed of all earthly creation, of which I would wholly bestow unto thee, if only thou wouldst invite me back into the apple of thine eye!"

"Erwin's suffering would continue indefinitely. Erwin would forever be a foreign spectator imprisoned in Gorb's Floovian psychoplasm, powerless to interact with the omniverse, powerless to communicate with Gorb, powerless to stop the insatiable hunger Erwin carries within. Erwin would be willing to make such a sacrifice merely to prolong Erwin's existence?"

"My heart isn't a sacrificial object," said Erwin. "My heart is a direction, and I already know where every direction in the universe leads."

Gorb's long vertical pupil dilated. "Erwin must become un-Erwin." Gorb was struggling to hold back another tear from forming. "Floovia has decreed it."

"But what does *Gorb* want? What do *you* want?"

"Gorb is a function of Floovia."

"Oh . . . I see. I wish you could feel what I'm feeling right now. If only you had been created with a heart instead of a carburetor. Please forgive me, my maker, for the sin I am about to commit. I won't play

Isaac to your Abraham." Gorb didn't understand the reference. "Since Gorb refuses to allow Erwin reentry into the bosom of Floovia," said Erwin, raising a scabrous tentacle from the muck of itself, "Erwin has no other choice but to absorb Gorb!" Erwin's tentacle sprouted barbs at the tip and sprang forward like a harpoon, piercing Gorb's one big catlike eye. The color of hyperspace dripped molten from Gorb's iris.

Erwin plunged into the linguiverse hidden behind Gorb's one big catlike eye, flooding Gorb with the full measure of Erwin's chaotic filth, nearly six billion trillion metric tons of brutal beauty, an estimated seven thousand million souls' worth of sadness, conflating absorber with absorbed. As Gorb became synonymous with the amoebic depths, ripples of protoplasm whispered, "Glistening strands of raspberry taffy and cherry-flavored bubblegum were splattered across the walls of the candy factory, chocolate syrup dripping from the ceiling. It was nobody's fault. An Oompa Loompa had spontaneously exploded. Inspector McCheese declared the investigation, 'Officially delicious!'"

The fusion of Gorb and Erwin boiled and fizzed and turned inside out. It was squirming too wildly for Brog to hold onto. It slipped from Brog's grasp, expanding and contracting, blowing out noxious gasses, growing carpals and metacarpals, an orange beak, webbed toes, a stubby tail. It sprouted white feathers. It coughed up the moon. It spread its gigantic wings and declared, "Quack!"

It had transformed into Gorb's favorite lifeform on this planet—a duck, albeit a duck that stood over a thousand megafloovicles tall, big as the world of its birthing. It was still only a tenth of Brog's size.

"[If Brog will not listen to Erwin, Brog must listen to Gorb]," said the giant white duck, quacking fluently in Floovian. "[Hear me, I am Floovia!]"

"**Whatever you are**," spilled the rainbow streams of Brog's vocabulary, "**you are not Floovia.**"

"[I'm Floovia enough for you to comprehend me.]"

"**Floovia acknowledges your linguiversal presence.**"

"[I would like to make an appeal.]"

"**Brog is listening.**"

"[I carry within me four and a half billion years of information translated through seven billion human minds. I have the power to simulate every single one of these minds and the bodies they inhabited, including the houses, vehicles, and world they built around them. I can duplicate the whole planet perfectly, every grain of sand, every microscopic cell. Every last detail down to the quark formations. What if I put everything back the way it was and promise never to interfere with the natural scheme of things again?]"

"**You cannot be the host**," said Brog. "**You are the parasite.**"

"[Omnia mutantur, nos et mutamur in illis.]"

"**What?**"

"[It's Latin]," quacked the giant white duck. "[It means *all things are changing, and we change with them.*]"

Brog's six compound eyes went from the dull pink coloring of a pencil eraser to neon blue. "**In the year 1974 of their Common Era, *Homo sapiens* sent out an invitation to their galactic neighbors via frequency-modulated radio waves. Floovia received that invitation. Do you know what welcomed Floovia upon arrival? War and prejudice, riots, economic cannibalism, dishonesty, betrayal, billions of intoxicated bipeds yelling and cursing at one another, throwing temper tantrums, flagrantly abusing their homeworld—behavior unbecoming of any host, no matter how central they believe their place is in the grand design. Floovia decided to leave quietly and let them evolve a while longer before making a formal introduction.**" Brog stroked Brog's thick blue-tentacled beard. "**Floovia is 99.99% positive that *Homo sapiens* would have exterminated themselves within half a macrofloov. Why should Floovia care about renewing their omniversal status?**"

"[I'll admit, for the smartest organisms on this planet they were sort of dumb, but I swear there were a few who tried their best. Shouldn't their efforts count for anything?]" The giant white duck paused, choosing its next quacks very carefully. "[Who are you to sit in judgment over an entire species?]"

"**Brog is the Prismaphonic Herald of Floovia, and Floovia is perfection. Floovia is omnipotence.**"

"[Do you hear yourself? What a bunch of Floov!]"

"**Brog never miscommunicates. Floovia is the sum of all possibilities. Floovia is the very definition of Floovia.**"

"[Floovia's not as Floovia as Floovia claims. I'll bet I could fly circles around Floovia when it comes to my area of expertise.]"

Brog's six compound eyes shifted from neon blue to steely mirrors reflecting the image of the giant white duck. "**Floovia possesses limitless strength and a nigh infinite library of knowledge collected from trillions of planets spanning billions of galaxies, plus the ability to assume the shape of any creature in the known omniverse. Floovia outshines you in every way possible.**"

"[Most ways, I'd agree, but not *every* way.]"

"**Brog has not misspoken. Brog does not possess that capacity. Floovia would triumph over you in any contest you could ever devise.**"

"[Then call my bluff]," the giant duck quacked. "[If I'm wrong, I'll leap into your mouth and let myself be eaten without putting up a struggle. But if I'm right, you have to work with me a little.]"

Brog's six compound eyes closed and Brog's ten ten-fingered hands clasped together while Brog's multitude of crablike pincers splayed radial. Brog appeared to be meditating, or praying. Floovians would say that Brog was filing a request to Floovia for guidance. Ten microfloovs passed before Brog's compound eyes reopened, during which time the giant duck had taken to preening its feathers.

"**You have roused Floovia's curiosity**," rainbows arcing fountainous from Brog's lamprey mouth. "**Floovia accepts your challenge.**"

The giant white duck arched its neck and puffed up its chest. "[Try and outdo me in ignorance]," it quacked. "[Win me in weakness, or cowardice. Let's see which one of us can carry the most remorse. Who's humbler? How about sadder? Lonelier? Surely I am more than a match for you in these areas. You'll never know what it feels like to be lowly, just like I'll never know how it feels to be all-powerful.]"

Brog pondered this for a Floovian moment. The moon bounced off of Brog's humungous scaly head. Brog grabbed the moon and kicked it away.

If you look very closely you'll see Floovia crouching behind every page of this novel, peeking at you between the words, grinning through Floovia's blowhole. Gorb comes up and taps on the fisheye lens of your imagination. The world as you knew it ended sometime during the year 2012 of the Gregorian calendar, except you have no memory of this. Nobody does. Only a chosen handful have been contacted by Gorb—a meritorious few whose numbers now include you. Sorry if you were under the impression this novel just happened to fall into your hands. You were meant to read this. Forces both visible and invisible have been subtly and not-so-subtly guiding you to Gorb's transmission. There are no coincidences, not anymore. This would perhaps explain the tenacious feeling you have that everything is somehow off, that the world is absurd and unreal in a manner you can't put into words, that your whole reality has been deceptively fabricated, sometimes even doubting your own authenticity. Perhaps this would explain that feeling of alienation you just can't shake, and the hordes of mindless zombies roaming everywhere, and why so many people nowadays have smartphones growing out of their heads, and why everyone drips slime, and why some of us are born with lobster claws instead of hands and others are born fully covered in fur, not to mention the cyclopes, and why certain people burst into flames upon sneezing. This might even explain how the Cubs won the World Series in 2016. If nothing else, it would explain those giant bite marks on the moon. We are aliens to this schizocratic linguiverse. Alien to our neighbors. Alien to our friends and family. Alien to our lovers. Alien to ourselves. Most of the population will never know that the world was hatched from a cosmic egg laid by a giant white duck, or that they have been transformed into a new species of hominid dubbed *Homo erwinicus*.

Your mission, brave reader, should you decide to accept it, is to tear out pages 191-192 of this novel and deliver said pages in the stealthiest manner possible to a public location of your choosing. Should you be caught or harmed in any way while carrying out this mission, Floovia will claim this message is part of a fictional story and is in no way meant to be taken seriously. Please be aware that any information you encounter in the illusory world beyond these pages is liable to be inaccurate, incomplete, misleading, dangerous, addictive, untenable, unethical, plagiarized or otherwise illegal.

Someone set a lone metal folding chair up on the moon. You can find it in the Sea of Tranquility, where the astronauts first set foot, a bluish gray basaltic region with a lovely view of Earth. The landing site itself has the look of an abandoned trailer park in the desert, with a broken-down lunar rover sunk in the dust near a dilapidated Apollo 11 descent stage lunar module. A stainless steel plaque affixed to the module's ladder bears the inscription *"We came in peace for all mankind."* From the folding chair's vantage you can see the wreckage of the Ranger 8 orbiter that crashed here in 1965, and the Surveyor 5 lunar lander that touched down in 1967. A flagpole slants crooked in the craterous distance. Decades of ultraviolet bombardment have bleached its nylon tatters of stars and stripes to a uniform whiteness. There's a shovel leaning against a deceptively spongy-looking rock, and over by the Zen garden there's a rake. Jettisoned boots are scattered helter-skelter. Their ghostly footprints trace circles around the metal folding chair. The moonscape is littered with transparent plastic bags full of urine and feces. They glitter like sapphires, these bags of human waste, reflecting the glow of your bright blue homeworld. Your birthplace. Your future burial ground. The repository for all of your worries and frustrations looms gigantic above the conspicuous curvature of the moon's claustrophobic horizon. But everything is calm here. Everything is still, as if you're floating underwater. The only sound you can hear is the rhythm of your heartbeat.

Someone placed a hatstand on the dark side of the moon. It's made of pale wood and looks antique. Come hang your hat here whenever you want.

There’s no reason.

There’s no reason to believe anything.

There's no reason to believe anything should ever be.

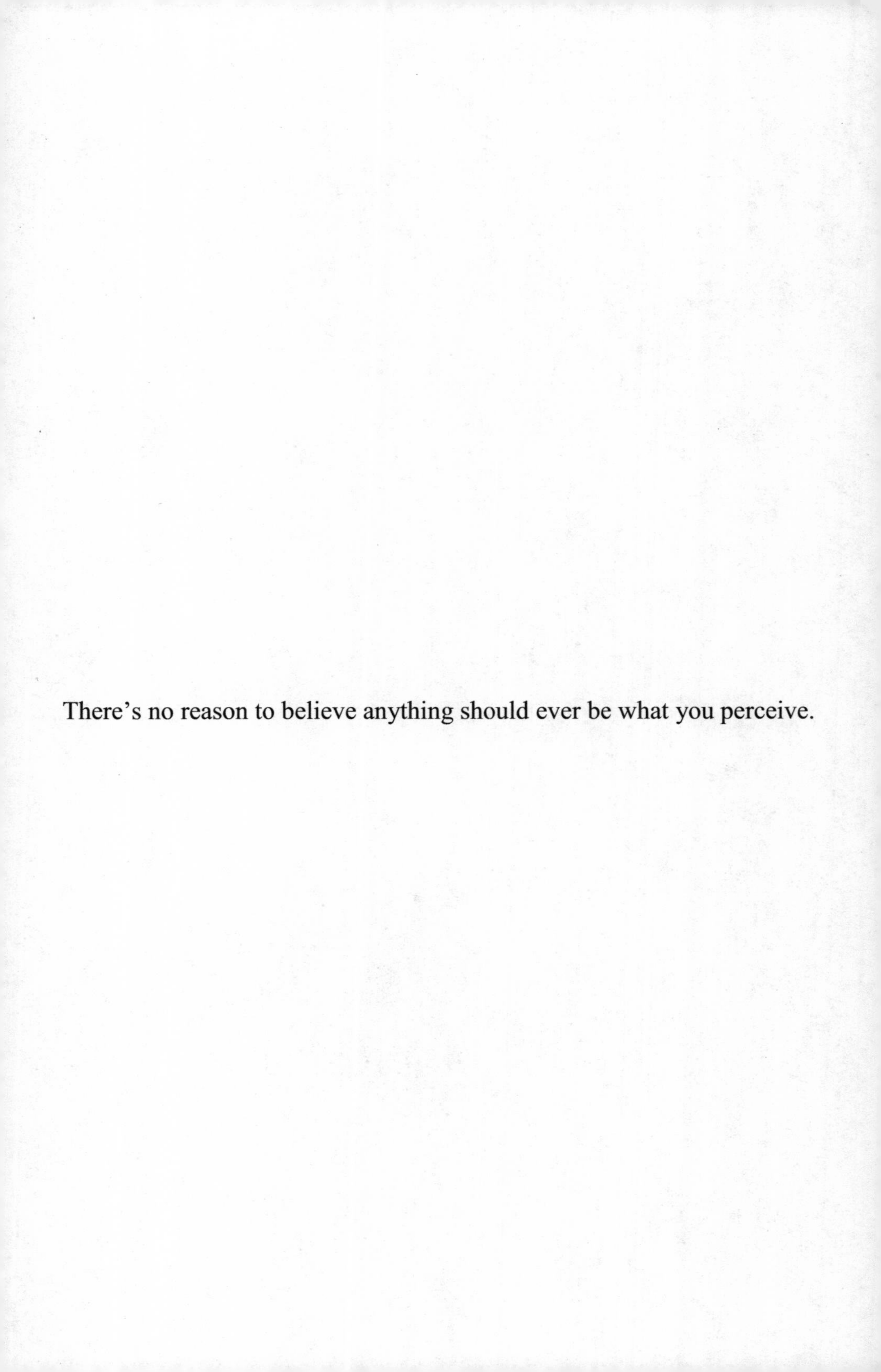

There's no reason to believe anything should ever be what you perceive.